Christmas Stones
&
The Story Chair

Justin Isherwood

Photographed & Designed
by
Mary "Casey" Martin

Published by
Home Brew Press

Several of these stories first appeared in the *Stevens Point Journal*.

FIRST EDITION -December 1999
ISBN 1-891609-07-6 Hardcover
ISBN 1-891609-04-1 Softcover

LIBRARY OF CONGRESS CARD CATALOG NUMBER
99-076685
Cataloging-in-Publication Data
Isherwood, Justin
Christmas Stones & The Story Chair / Justin Isherwood - 1st ed.
Title.
Fiction. Christmas. Agriculture. Wisconsin. History.

DESIGNER / EDITOR / PHOTOGRAPHER
Mary "Casey" Martin

Marketed & Published by
HOME BREW PRESS
A Micro-Brewery of Words & Art
2540 Abby Lane P.O. Box 185
Wisconsin Rapids WI
54495-0185
MARY "CASEY" MARTIN, PUBLISHER
PH/FAX: 715.421.2429
ORDERS PH/FAX: 800.250.2986
VOICE/PAGER: 888.492.4531
EMAIL: mcm@wctc.net

Dedication

to the keeper of my house and my heart

Christmas Stones
& The Story Chair

Justin Isherwood

Table of Contents

Christmas Stones & The Story Chair

Introduction

Survival and Christmas are not to the modern mind co-dependent. I was born to a place where Christmas was rendered possible because within the host of my family burned an old and somewhat curious instinct.

My family has been in the Wisconsin since 1832. Not in itself anything peculiar, for we came to Wisconsin desirous as every emigrant. To have at last that most compelling of resources, indeed the bravest, most dear thing any farmer can want, dear it be as blood itself. And if there is ever a religion true to what farmers are true to . . . on that altar shall be a meager pile of earth, common dirt, and to it shall members of the congregation with their big knuckled hands pledge eternal fidelity. We, my family, came to Wisconsin for land, not wee patches of it, not land at the laird's say so, land not as crofters and tenants, but land in big gleaming tracts, land at once and forever our own.

So it happened, as is the consequence of being farmers, and our relationship with dirt, already profound if not quite metaphysical, became more so because as farmers we are required to plow, harrow, disc, hoe, pick rock, dig post holes, dig graves, tend deeper streams. Did I mention pick rock, also pick potatoes, bury dogs, and dig cellars? The result of all this upheavel was a collection.

Every one of them thought it foolish and did not admit to friend or stranger that they were, though mature and god-believing, still doing that old thing, collecting stones. Stones in pockets and cheese boxes, stones on window sills, stones in tool boxes, stones on upright pianos, stones given to girlfriends, stones on the kitchen table, stones to hold at church when what was being said and sung didn't quite match what was real. It was inevitable that this zeal for stones did soon enough begin to tell stories, stone stories. An altogether excessive thing considering every story was at its core nothing more than an ordinary stone. A common kind of stone with no breeding, no bloodline, no true value other than it had been in some sod buster's pocket a fair good while since he found it at the plowing. My family, by itself, was not of a kind to exaggerate. We were Methodees and for that kind, exaggeration was a mortal sin the same as dancing and tea. What happened was the stone's fault, rumbling and ribald in the "overhaul" pocket, and the man's fingers felt upon it every time he went to his pocket knife, every match, there was that stone gathering round his fingers.

Nobody but a farmer knows how a stone can whisper from a pocket, take up a chant, break into lyrics, rondels, rhymed verse and it the only companion of the farmer that day of long rows in endless number. Was only right and natural my family did listen to stones, and because so, hear the story. None of which would have mattered but for Christmas, as wasn't our fault, Merry Christmas was someone else's fault. Ours was in allowing the stones to talk.

It is the well-known and standing obligation of farmers to bring to Christmas a separate perspective than has their cousin in the village. The reasons are complex and have to do with why there are farmers in the first place when cleaner work and better wages are to be had in the suburbs. It is for Christmas to bind up the family to what is and what matters. To this came the stones, stories that if told in other places might be thought unkind, perhaps even cruel, but to our place, our lot, our earth, a story that marked our need. Story enough to embolden us, this the farmer kind, as must go beyond the babe in the feedbox. It was not quite good enough that shepherds were said to have heard singing in the hills. My family needed to hear the singing for themselves, not rumors of singing. We were not satisfied with distant tales of a stable; we needed more than to visit the place for we had done chores there.

It helped that my family has always lived in the rural dominion, at a distance from the village, its manners, and a tissue-wrapped kind of Christmas. My family gave work gloves for Christmas, also barn rubbers, a new manure fork, a wax ring for the toilet. We cut our tree from the woods, the ice cream was made from ice chopped free of the stock tank. Christmas done right, according to the honor-code of my family, was done on the cheap, and a few slices less than cheap might better prove the point.

That Christmas came to be acutely focused on stones was no accident. We were after all Celts for whom stones have a certain kindredness. There is to stones something implicitely eternal, some measure, if awkward and sundry, of the divine, which any seminarian knows is not how the divine is supposed to comport itself. My family did not read horoscopes, tea leaves, the palms of their hands, or make inquiry regarding their fate in the guts of chickens; we did, however, listen to stones. Luck for us never ran in a rabbit's foot, never grew in the clover. If luck is to be found, it is in a stone.

Stones is what we called them, the stories. The older among us called them stanes. I have collected a few of the stone stories. I apologize to those who shall not find these stones becoming of Christmas, but they are not farmers.

Ours was a Christmas that must do more than bind people to each other, for its task was also to bind people to land in a way that is entirely unmodern, during times when there are a thousand better reasons to forsake the farm than continue. In the stones my family heard their creed and some explanation, however rudimentary, why they were farmers in the first place. The reasons are silly in any casual light, a backward sentiment, a reason if examined would be found heretical; that is, profoundly pagan. Here was exposed the centering substance of those who farm. What word utters this meaning to those who belong is in the ancient tongue, "uir," a primitive sound but sufficient. That word later became "uirta," in time successfully misspelled again to become . . . "earth."

If other places must center their Christmas on the

cradle, a star, a stable . . . my kind gathered around a more familiar metaphor, a stone. A stone held in the hand, warmed in the circle of our collective innocence and from this rose a story, given voice by the throats of uncles who were not normal or literary.

It was an ordinary stone, a common kind of aggregate, that we blessed with the line "and this no ordinary stone is . . ." This how it always began.

The Story Chair

Custom in my family is to tell stories at Christmas. Specifically stone stories, tales whose nativity and metaphor, narrative and scene, faithfulness and tone, are rooted in what appears to the casual observer a stone, an unremarkable stone, a casual stone and ordinary chunk of rock. Every year the great uncles, the ruminating and hoary uncles, rise from their arthritic reliquaries to wage war, wage it once more with and on each other. Story war.

True, they said, this bout of eye-gouging, blood-letting stone-wrestling began a long time before, in some misremembered place that probably isn't there anymore. This, the trait that has continued, unabated, generation by generation, age by age, epoch by epoch, at every Christmas since. Every year the greaking auld gars shuffle their way to the story seat and once keen and settled on its altar, unwind in outrageous, immaculate detail, the full and sometimes uncured pelt of a story whose incubation was a stone.

As a child, I was surrounded by all manner of uncles, batches and hatches of uncles, collects and coliseums of uncles, moraines and munificences of uncles, heaps and humongouses of uncles, piles and penduncals of uncles, some of whom were aunts, also grandmothers, mothers-in-law, sisters, and a hop girl or two. Every year we gathered, every Christmas as if by some galvanic chemistry, gathered to hear the stone. The only requirement to this earnest competition was the stone; no pencils, feathers or safety pins, no jackknives, headdresses or boat anchors. I don't know why but that was the rule. Gold counted if in nugget form, this how it happened Uncle George ventured a telling of the Klondike back in '85, how it happened the three fingers on his left hand were rounded off by frostbite. All the while holding in his hand a chunk of that winking ore the size of a pigeon egg.

I don't know why or who first passed the rule, but there it was, every story vented, to be preceded and annotated by a stone, and this same stone passed around those who heard it. Nay ordinary stone as any could see, handed around it was like a hallowed relic from some ravished monastery. So it was the most commonplace, sundry and ordinary stone, when served up with story, became a thing sanctified. Every child in the circle of this stone's breath . . . and surely we knew that stones did breathe same as a person or cow breathes only slower, more patient. Every child in the telling circle learned of the far murks from which our kind had come. Ordinary folk we were, till the stone was added, the resulting new mixture of us told from the place anointed; meaning the chair.

As a result, every child of us had a hundred stories to tell, not of blue ox or Crockett, but Great Great Great Uncle George off to the Klondike and how half the way he walked, the other half he wished he had. The story exhumed in excruciating detail from the recesses of the archeological abyss. Redeemed instantly, full length, and in technicolor, all by placing a stone in the hand of one who in their own long before sat cross-legged on the floor and heard the story. By what spell, what medium this came about I do not know, for it defies reason that a stone, a mere piece of agregate, of sedimentation, fossil, horn, coral, greenstone, granite, brick, soap stone, bone, and creek bottom pebble, could raise forth from the depths of ancestral incognito the precise, full-scale heroic ruin of it all.

By placing a stone in hand was the dullest narration transformed. Same as Great Uncle Henry's wife, who was a foreigner from Missouri, who belonged to a religious theatre, who in arousal commenced to speak in tongues. Nothing was beyond her, neither extraterrestrial dialect nor bushman babble nor phonemes of Australopithicus africanis (which was a long time ago). We well understood. For by a similar trick was every creaking andeluvian relic of an uncle and moribund aunt transubstantiated. These virtuous, choir-singing aunts, who by placing a stone in their hand, did espouse a most notorious legend. All in the first person, and at the simple employ of a stone.

Still to do the story right it was required to enthrone the teller. How long the story seat had been part of the annual incantation I can not say. Some have said

Ethlred of Saxons once reposited on this very same implement, though it didn't look quite that old. In fact it resembled a kitchen chair as suffered a head-on collision with delirium, before us was more a vehicle than a chair. Some believed it was more the chair talking than the hulks of uncles who under ordinary circumstances could not connect two thoughts much less a story with subplots and elusive motive.

A curious artifact was it, one leg blue, one leg orange, another of a hue commonly left to chicken gizzards, while the fourth was ebonized as if from conflagration. A stool it was more than a chair, though it appeared to have once been a chair.

Every Christmas this chair was brought forth from the closet of its holy keeping. Set with ceremony in the circle of the collect. In order of their penultimate ancestry, each great uncle did take seat and bring forth from his pocket the most boastful, most glorious, most literary stone. On the story chair they sat and slowly turned the narrative in their terrible wounded hands, the chair greetching and sweating beneath them.

A most unusual chair was it, this story chair. In all creation there was none else like it. More museum than chair, for attached to it was all manner of artifact. Strange gryphon beasts slunk from its recesses, a pocket knife enshrined, and statues of saints not known elsewhere. There were bullets of Antitem and Shiloh embedded, a strange copper winding, a tiny silver casket, a feather, a blade of grass, a perfectly round stone, an arrowhead, a cigar butt last smoked by U.S. Grant, several nails, an axe head, a shilling, a page from the Bible . . . all these things and more affixed to this half-witted chair.

Despite its wounded appearance, it was a most imposing monument, it might be said a studpendous chair. If not remarkable and fabulous, surely an uplifting sort of chair, a prosperous, nearly pontifical chair, also a haunting and mystical chair, and too, a prosaic chair, and of course a Christmas chair. Every Christmas it was fetched from the closet and set in the center of my grandmother's parlor. This the only chair I ever knew that drooled. And if you listened close, it whinnied quite like the too-old plough horse hoping to be once again in the harness.

In my family it was this chair that raised us up and made stories of us, despite we were no else but farm folk. When set in our midst, the noise of us ceased, children unaccountably grew quiet, menfolk hushed their politics. Wars, if there were some, went off so far in the distance as to momentarily stop. In the presence of this chair it seemed all creation slowed and drew near with us. The cows listened, the trees crept close crowded with expectant birds, the children folded their knees beneath their chins-- all waiting to hear. Jupiter was seen eavesdropping at the window.

Every Christmas it was so. The story chair was brought forth, set in the center of the parlor and the stories began . . . Great Great Uncle Jim rose from us, slowly gathered himself to the chair and with agonizing slowness, sat down. From the pocket of his Sunday overalls he drew a stone and commenced, "This no ordinary stone is, it is the very stone, the exact and precise stone of one called Black Sparrow Hawk, more commonly known as Black Hawk, he of the Sauk and Fox . . ."

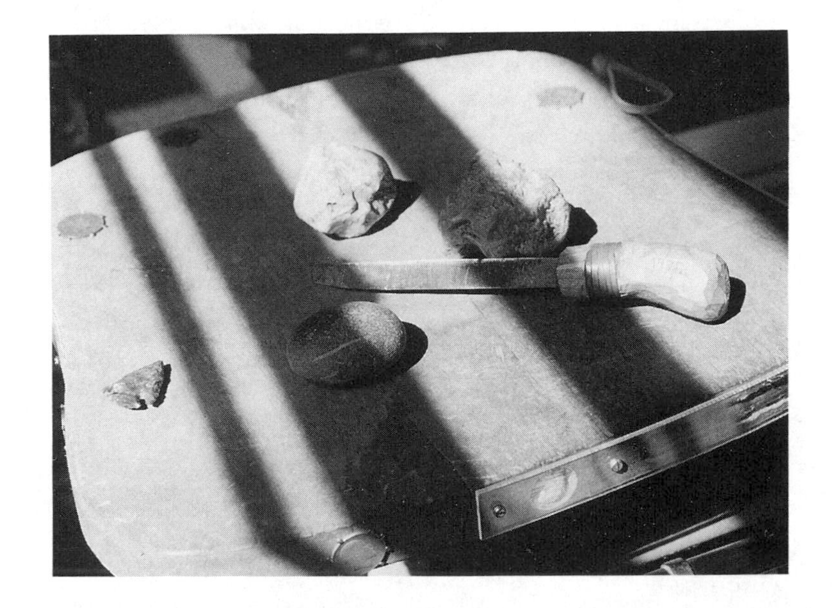

This My Children

Three of them were they: Jim, Edward, George. Four was Henry; he didn't farm, wore a tie, he lived in Missouri, not just down the road like them, the brothers. Story stones begins with them because they were cheap, and because they hated each other. Hate is what farmers have for without hate there can be no agricultural progress. George hated Jim for his silo. They together hated Edward for his potato digger despite the taters dug with it weren't worth the price of a new machine.

Economics on the farm is not the same as ecomonics in the village. Cash, should it exist, is first deployed to keep the farmstead impoverished to any new device as might be available, each of these in turn claiming to hold for agriculture more profitable days. That this doesn't happen is because another new machine is there to intercede the cash flow.

It is incumbent on every farmer to build a barn twice the size needed, half to hold the cows, the other half to impress the neighborhood. Same rule applies to the granary and the woodpile, all done to bring the neighbor to bankruptcy a fortnight before the instigator goes belly-up himself. This is why the brothers hated each other; they could not buy a roll of barbwire without their next over kin purchasing the gold-plated model. It was the same with everything; every hardware bolt, horse collar, pump handle and lightning rod was in competition. The final competition among Jim, Edward and George was Christmas. Uncle Henry didn't count.

As fate did contrive, these relic scrooges were my grandfather and great uncles, none who believed in Christmas as store-bought. No dolls, no buggies, no wind-up cars, no lethal-looking BB guns leering with loathsomeness. They, in self-defense, saying it wasn't their fault, for it had always been so. Christmas dependent not on the cookie jar or the pocketbook; besides they had just spent the last cash money on a new sulky plow. Instead, Christmas waged by their stories and their stones.

Wasn't they who started it, having been this way since Beowulf and MacDonald of Sleet, this way and ever so since MacAdam. Christmasing was to one purpose and this the stone; every Christmas since the Jacobites it's been just so, stones. Every Christmas they, the uncles, Jim, Edward and George and Henry also, he of Missouri, came to the house bearing in their barn coats an object wrapped in tissue. Except 'e of Missouri who wore a tie and a white shirt. Everyone knowing already it was nothing other than a stone, that we might in the exhaltation of Christmas unwrap. 'Course it was a stone. A fist-size, good-for-nothing, worthless, dim-witted stone. Some were green, some round, some square, some curved and oblate. Some had holes in them or looked bitten, others were glassy or perfect cannonballs or had almost pictures in them if you looked just right. Still they were stones, dumb stones, not nearly as good as an erector set or Red Ryder BB gun.

After supper on Christmas night my uncles settled themselves on the seat of an embellished, if not altogether entombing, chair and in the hushed quiet and principled dark of new winter's eve, each in turn did take up the stone. The very one unwrapped to groaning disappointment. Holding it thus in their hand, each began the telling of the story, how this was not a stone after all, rather something so very other than a stone. Thus it was always, now as in the time of the MacKays and MacMillans, also MacDonald and MacGregor, when stones were told by the Lord of the Isles himself on his Christmas night. These great chiefs, my uncles and grandfather, sat by the fire telling stones and by this have we thrived all the family long. Thrived, for not being . . . store-bought.

I knew my uncles were cheap, white-maned lairds though they be, and grandfather, too. What I wanted, truly, was a BB gun, not a stone story, yet I sat at their feet as they, with a blanket over their knees, held up their stone and began the story. Each had practiced his stone to be better and more intricate than the others. These three who couldn't otherwise tell the day of the week had rehearsed this one story over the plough handles since spring. Knew it by heart to every syllable and ripple and became like the rime-makers of old, so very good as to be . . . almost . . . store-bought.

Each of them in the order of their birth, Jim,

Edward, George and Henry, held the stone in their worn hands under the buttermilk light of the farmhouse. Each trying to out-tell the other, their voices going smoky and shamanistic, merlins with words, alchemists who did strive to turn stone . . . into . . . store-bought.

And Jim began, "This my children no ordinary stone is . . . about Ekbod the Giant who dwelt in the Land of Dune that was over from Dunfris and Kilmarnock. A loathsome giant was he standing eight foot seven. Ekbod was neither wise nor daft; many had ventured his land to outwit him thinking always, as folk do, that giants have wee tiny brains, same as dinosaurs, and are clumsy and web-footed besides. Not Ekbod. He, while no Einstein, was neither a simp, and when a chrome-plated warrior came to joust with him, certain of his own agility as proven in combat with dragons and wizards, thinking he had but to draw his regal sword and let the light glint from it, then would Ekbod yield . . . were they ever mistaken. Ekbod did however bury them decently. Which is better than had they won. They'd have severed Ekbod the Giant's head with a dull saw and taken it home in a potato sack to display, so as not to drag it in the dirt on the way. Ekbod dug them a deep grave safe from wolves, if sometimes villagers disinterred the freckless knight to recycle his armor and claim the socks.

"So it was after awhile that no one came to challenge Ekbod the Giant who lived in the Land of Dune and this might have been fine enough any other place but the Land of Dune was special. Round about were the lands of Clay, Cobble and Hardscrabble; they were not particularly good lands. Surely they were selfish lands, whereby a crofter with a good back in him and children did bare survive. While in the Land of Dune was good sandy loam and through its middle coursed the River Jewel. In Dune a mannie could with only a short hoe, tend his taties and bagies, his neeps and kale and soon after grow fat and shiny. Besides, the Land of Dune was sheltered by the Mountains of Loom, that on hot days, about four o'clock, the sun went beheck the peaks and the land cooled so by bedtime a person might sleep. Not so the Lands of Clay, Cobble and Hardscrabble. There the dust never settled and the mud never quit, and it was both too hot and too cold at the same time, so pitiful even the Farmer's Almanac couldn't make sense of it. Ekbod the Giant might have shared his domain in the Land of Dune but he did not think it the sort of thing a giant ought do; he had his reputation after all. If people around knew he was a vegetarian and really didn't suck the marrow of his victims, instead giving them a good Episcopalian service from the Book of Prayer, there'd be no end to the challengers waiting at this gate. Especially the psychological types who'd study the game films and research his moves and hope one day to land a lucky thrust killing Ekbod same as that pipsqueak who killed off his distant cousin Goliath."

At this juncture Uncle Jim turned over in his hands what looked to be a brick-shaped stone.

"There was in the Land of Cobble a boy named Weasle, so named because he was lithe and slight. Weasle did not under ordinary circumstance cast a shadow, and any time after dusk he became completely invisible. Weasle did not wish to remain a weasle all his life, he wanted like everyone else to grow fat and so round they'd call him Woodchuck, or Falstaff, or something noteworthy and well-fed. Weasle also wished to marry and in the Land of Cobble as in Clay and Hardscrabble a young man without substance could not marry until such a time as he could support his darling. This was ever so much worse than practicing safe sex.

"Weasle too might have joined the list of those errants who wound their way to Ekbod's portal gate to shout up their challenge that Ekbod come forth and fight. Weasle knew his limitations better than most, so he did not bargain for armor plate at the pawn shop. Instead he thought and thought and thought some more until an idea came to him of how he might conquer the Land of Dune. Then he thought some more, for this a very wise person must do to appreciate the liabilities of a great idea. And he thought and he thought and he thought until he had a plan that would have worked with his hands tied behind his back, which of course it must, since this was part of his plan.

"Little Weasle searched the castle walls of Ekbod every night, climbing them stone by stone, studying the workmanship and the mortar mix. It was a very well built wall of stout big stones, only here and there did the masons cheat a little and place a small stone among the boulders. All of them high quality save one, this the one he was looking for. This very stone."

Uncle Jim held up the brick-shaped stone. "This the exact very same stone Weasle chiseled out with a tiny wood mallet, for the giant must not hear him, and pried with a screwdriver until the stone came free, and through the hole he could see into the castle's keep.

"The next night Weasle returned to the castle of Ekbod, removed the brick-shaped stone and one by one placed in the opening the contents of the bag tied across his shoulders. The second night he did the same. And the next. For two weeks he did likewise. Two months went by before Weasle returned to Ekbod's castle in the Land of Dune. This time he carried with him climbing spurs and a coil of rope. He was not halfway up the wall making more noise than he ought when the rope he was hanging on was suddenly jerked over the top of the wall and he found himself staring eye to eye with Ekbod the Giant. He noticed how much bigger Ekbod's face was than his and how he had bad breath and looked haggard from lack of sleep.

"*'So you came to die little man,'* said Ekbod. With a flourish surprising in a person his size he tied Weasle up with the very same rope Weasle used to scale the castle. *'Tomorrow morning,'* Ekbod roared, *'I'll crack your bones and eat you.'* Never mind Ekbod wouldn't do that, preferring porridge and brown sugar but he had his image to protect.

"That night in the dungeon Weasle heard Ekbod tramping around the castle, making sounds on the floor only a giant can. Apparently things weren't going well with Ekbod. Weasle heard him breaking dishes, chasing something with a broom, swatting the floor, shouting in frustration. After awhile Ekbod went to bed but was soon up again, swatting at the floor with another broom.

"Weasle, who could whistle very well, began to do so, at which the giant shouted down from his bed chamber that Weasle should cease immediately or die, instead of waiting until morning.

"Like he hadn't heard Ekbod, Weasle continued whistling and soon the giant shouted down another warning.

"'*Stop or die, little one.*'

"Weasle persisted. He whistled Gypsy Rover, Boat Song, Amazing Grace, and when he couldn't think of another repeated them. Shortly he heard Ekbod rise from his bed, snatch up his buckle and sword and descend the dark stair to the dungeon, Weasle was still whistling.

"'*Are you deaf, pipsqueak? Did you not hear my warning!,*' exploded Ekbod.

"Weasle only smiled and whistled despite his lips were very sore. As Ekbod struggled to find the keys to the cell Weasle said in a comforting voice, '*I see you don't sleep so well?*'

"'*What's it to you, short stuff?*'

"'*Well, good giant, because I can fix that.*'

"'*The heck you can speck because you're gonna be jam in but a moment and tomorrow I'm gonna spread my toast with your remains.*' The very rhetoric upset Ekbod's stomach as he uttered these words.

"'*And if I die, you will sleep just as badly tomorrow night and even worse every night thereafter because the solution, dear giant, will die with me.*'

"Ekbod stared at Weasle. With his one good eye he studied the wee one, like a giraffe might look over a mouse.

"*Listen, dust mite,*' said Ekbod, '*you haven't the foggiest what's bothering me. You're just trying to avoid the obvious.*'

"*'Dear giant, here be I, bound hand and foot, and you suspect me of treachery? If you could but unbind my feet I shall by the time the sun rises fix your problems.'*

"*'But immeasurable iota, you don't even know what is bothering me.'*

"*'I know that it is bothering you enough that you will let me try.'*

"*'Oh alright, you microscopic inconsequence. I will untie your feet but still I shall fix a lanyard about your waist and keep the coil at my feet so if you try to escape I shall snatch you up and burst your spine quicker than you can blink and you will be toast.'* With this he unbound Weasle who immediately leaped to his feet and began dancing a slow ancient kilt song. Whistling all the while.

"*'Must you whistle,'* shouted Ekbod.

"*'Sorry gigantic master, I must.'* Weasle whistled up the dungeon stairs trailing the rope behind, whistled throughout the castle, going from room to room, tip-toeing through the guard towers, danced across the bailey, all the dances he knew, waltzes and soft shoes, tangos and sambas. In the darkness a scurrying sound arose, hundreds of tiny feet were following him and when he went up the sentry walk to the top of the castle wall, a thousand more followed, lured by the whistling Weasle. And when he lept over the parapet they leaped also, tens of thousands of itsy-bitsy feet.

"A mighty jerk on the rope roused Ekbod for he had fallen most asleep. Blast if that little frit wasn't trying to escape, and with a mighty snatch he reeled in Weasle from the depths of the watery moat which was a good thing seeing Weasle was hand-bound and could not swim.

" 'Trying to escape, you inestimable nothing?"

" 'No Sire, was I not. Only to bring you relief and if you will but listen you will hear what I mean.'

"Ekbod did listen and did hear. Actually he did not hear, for they were gone. The rats that had suddenly overwhelmed his tidy castle were gone, so was their gnawing. His grain bags were safe and his sleep might once again be peaceful.

"The giant shook his mighty head saying he must sleep on this. He threw Weasle back into the cell, slammed the iron door and stumbled up the stairs.

"Weasle smiled to himself, though still rather uncomfortable as his arms were yet stoutly bound behind his back.

"Ekbod slept late that morning. When he did wake he took a slow breakfast and was about to begin eating when he thought of Weasle. Oh well, he said to himself, I ought to feed the little bugger. He wound his way to the dungeon, unlocked the cell, hoisted Weasle under one arm and hauled him up the stairs to the kitch. There he retied Weasle, poured a bowl the size of a washtub full of porridge, dressed it with raspberry jam which doesn't look pretty but tastes wonderful, pointed Weasle at it and they fell to eating. Weasle ate the entire bowl and had a loaf of toast besides."

Uncle Jim added how Weasle and Ekbod went into business together. How Ekbod married Weasle's sister and they had a ton of kids who kept Ekbod awake at night but he couldn't drown them as easy as the rats. And how Weasle married Ekbod's cousin from Thorsville who was considerably bigger than Weasle . . . and they had a ton of kids. Thereafter the Land of Dune raised potatoes and cabbage and they all lived pretty well, if not necessarily happy ever after.

"And this is the very exact same stone, the one Weasle chiseled from Ekbod's castle. A nice square stone, he could put back in its place each night after he dumped in more rats who had been altogether malnourished in the Land of Clay, Cobble and Hardscrabble. Ekbod surely would have noticed the hole had not Weasle neatly replaced the stone. A round stone wouldn't have stayed put, only this brick-shaped one; and this is the story."

Then it was Henry's turn.

Three Ravens

Uncle Henry, the Great Great Uncle Hen, went down-river on a lumber raft, went aground, and fought off pirates. In an unguarded moment he married a confederate woman who never came to visit being she was allergic to northerners.

Allergic to yankees, Uncle Henry said. A good dear woman is she, but devoted when it comes to a grudge. She being Missouri, that is to be expected.

Every year at Christmas the ancestral uncles sat down to tell their annual story. First came Uncle Jim who was some older than dirt and looked it. Then came Uncle Ed who lived in the yellow house on the school road with the best looking bay window in the township owing it faced the south and the kitchen table in it on any sunny winter afternoon, felt close to summer. After Uncle Ed came George and then Unc Henry of that unrepentant region.

Telling stories was serious to the brothers same

as chess is serious to others and sometimes Uncle Ed passed, which they could do, putting up George to tell his story and sometimes George passed too, meaning it was Uncle Henry's time. Being the babe of the family he couldn't pass, so straight on he commenced.

Uncle Henry slid the stool out in the middle of the room, and when the place touched quiet, reached underneath the stool and pulled forth a stone as resembled more an egg than a stone. He held the stone and slowly rotated it. On its face was a deep curving wound as if struck by a steel talon.

"Once in the kingdom of Indians lived a tribe who inhabited the high clay bluffs on the west shore of the Mississippi. They were a corn people whose lives had become settled and nice. As a result they gave up the chase, which wasn't very Indian of them. On the bluffs above the river they built a timber palisade around their village to make it safe from the jealous. Like the Aztecs of Mexico and the old Egyptians, they built pyramids. Great, looming, bureaucratic, tax-dollar pyramids of shagbark and willow, course on course of wattle laid down into which earth was hammered and the outside paved over with a layer of red clay.

"From a distance, both up stream and down, the red pyramids of the corn Indians were seen in sharp departure from the wild scene. They were of these mounds particularly proud, for no other people in all North America did raise such a monument, lofty and stern were these pyramids, dark against the sky, evidence the gods had granted to them the honor of being the overseer of all they surveyed. Being it was a particular high place, that domain was considerable. So it was without much interference from their conscience they did make slaves of other nations. Preyed on them by war, took by force their children and wives. Raided their fields, burnt their villages, because they were strong and because god so favored them.

"In a battle with a small band of Iowa, who weren't very warlike, the Red Clay people captured a young man by the name of Three Ravens, with the intent of sacrificing him on the stone altar as surmounted the top of their pyramid for the express purpose of bringing on the next crop of corn. Their favorite method of execution being to drive a square stick through the man's chest, which in all likelihood would smart for awhile.

"They did not know Three Ravens was the son of a prairie shaman and carried with him the 'boggle stone,' this the very one I hold in my hands.

"At the appointed time of Three Ravens' execution, he produced from his belt pouch this stone, the sacred rune stone given to him by his father. Holding it out, he stood before the crowd who had come to watch him die. *'In this stone are all the dreams of my people,'* he cried out. *'If you kill me, these dreams will escape, and having nowhere else to hide, will reside in you. And in your haunted sleep you will see visions that mean absolutely nothing to you, and your village will soon empty because your tribe will all go mad. Your crops will wither and die for no one shall water the corn. The rain will wash away the earth of your great mound. The walls of your village will rot and this place shall be empty of you . . . this, if you kill me, for I am the keeper of this stone. And if I crack the shell of this rock, all those dreams and alien nights will escape and you will not be rid of them until you are, every one, dead. So, wise People of the Corn, you must let me live. Release me back to my own kind!'* "

Uncle Henry held the stone of Three Ravens in his hand, rubbing it between his old fingers as if stroking a cat.

"What, dear Uncle, happened to the brave Three Ravens?" some child of us asked.

"They killed him. Five minutes after Three Ravens had warned them of his stone's power, he lay dead atop the great pyramid, a wooden spike the size of a fencepost driven through his chest. Gawd, how that must have smarted. The servants of the altar held his arms back as two muscled slaves positioned the stake over his chest, setting the point exact on his sternum, the stick already so sharp a pool of blood was forming in the dimple of the point pressing against his chest. On a nearby scafold stood a monster Indian with oiled arms completely naked except for an eye patch.

"*'Oh great!,'* thought Three Ravens, *'they are gonna kill me with a near-blind guy who will probably miss the stake and hammer one of the slave's heads to bits and I'll get splattered with the guy's brains and eyeballs, besides his runny nose, and then they will still kill me.'*

"He need not have worried, for the beautiful one-eye monster was an expert with the 38 pound mallet. He could swat a mosquito with it one handed, so good was he. He might have been a golf pro, had the game existed, and taken pleasure in killing an innocent white ball instead of hammering stakes through the hearts of neighbors to insure the corn crop.

"On the first stroke, the fencepost drove clean through Three Ravens' chest and his blood pressure went from 180 over 60 to zero in about as much time as it takes to say it. His brain winked out and his last thoughts were how it hardly smarted . . . he was almost going to think, 'wow,' but didn't have time.

"At this point the stone clutched in his hand, rolled away and one of the attending priests picked it up and in very excited tones pointed to the prominent scratch arcing across the stone's surface. *'The dreams are unleashed,'* he said, utterly panic-stricken. *'See for yourselves. There is the crack that Three Ravens warned of. A scratch where none before existed. I know for I inspected the rock myself. It was perfectly smooth but a moment ago.'*

"Another priest came up and, abruptly snatching the stone from the panicked priest said, *'You fool, this is but an ordinary stone. Do you not know we are the chosen people and only our stones have the power of heaven and of gods? Do not be so foolish.'*

"*'Foolish you think I am. Foolish? You did not see the stone beforehand. You do not know of what you are speaking. It had no mark on it. Now it is clearly incised. Something is released.'* The shaken priest was of course yelling so noisily that everyone in the crowd heard him and were soon upset at the premonition.

"*'Perhaps we could yet save the man,'* screamed the first priest. *'Get him to call back the dreams now released.'*

"They both turned to look at the sorry corpse of

Three Ravens from whom the last blood was slowly dripping, the rest already down the trough that led to the river and for a brief moment turned a six square foot patch of Mississippi red, then soon absorbed as was the life and consciousness of Three Ravens.

"The first priest was now entirely beside himself and had to be led down the steps of the pyramid raving like a lunatic, clutching the stone of Three Ravens. Sobbing and stumbling and quite a mess. Just before they got to the infirmary, the deranged priest turned and with a furious wind-up, threw the infected stone the length of the main street where it rolled to a stop in front of the pyramid. The second, more circumspect priest who'd seen all kinds of grandstanding in his day, wished he hadn't done that, for the people of the village saw for themselves how the stone had a wound on its face as if made by the talon of an enormous bird. A scratch on a rock where none had existed before. Surely Three Ravens had been a powerful shaman and they ought not have killed him for now the alien dreams of Three Ravens would come to them in their sleep, just as he prophesized, and drive them mad.

"Three years later the grand city of the Corn People was deserted, the enormous clay pyramid had begun to sag as the spring rain washed out a corner and no one was there to repair it. As foretold, the village people began having bad dreams, dreams they could not explain. 'Course neither could they explain the dreams they had before the arrival of Three Ravens' stone. Three Ravens had simply stated the obvious, the routine. They took it as something mystical. The tribe grew listless, their corn crop failed two years in a row because people weren't sleeping well and weren't diligent with their hoes.

"The first priest killed himself by leaping over the bluff into the muddy shallows of the Mississippi. On the way down he was thinking how very pleasant this all was and if they could ever figure out a way to do this and not get killed at the bottom they'd make millions. 'Course his thoughts ended there.

"The second and wiser priest saw what had happened to the attitude of the village, how this Iowa brave no smarter than joe-pye-weed had got the better of them. For he knew the trick, a very old trick about transforming vulnerability from the obvious victim to someone else. Three Ravens had died very well indeed and maybe they ought have been more careful and selective. Offering to sacrifice the first priest instead, who's expectation of calamity was not the sort of attitude a community needs to thrive. When the first corn crop failed, the wiser priest removed himself down the river by canoe one night. He left behind his priestly robe and feathers. Never mind it was just an ordinary crop failure; the people wouldn't listen, they had gathered up all kinds of conspiracy theories and the second priest knew the game was over.

"They would not have believed the truth had he told them. Besides, he was rather fascinated to see what would happen to a people, a secure, well-fed people who wanted very much to believe something is wrong with them when in fact nothing is. Coughs and colds became hauntings and curses. People died as routinely as before but now it was ever more mysterious. The whole town became listless and stupid, simple diaper rashes became portents, the people forgot their manners and panic took over.

"Of course he knew the cheap trick Three Ravens had performed, how he had taken up a pinch of mud and clay and smoothed this over the fissure in the stone so the first priest, on seeing the stone, believed it intact and unblemished. And then in the final moment of his life, he scratched away the clay filler, so when the stone rolled away from his dead hand it was an omen.

"If they had but examined the man's fingernails the clay filler was there to be seen. But nobody wanted to touch the body except at arm's length, and golly did they give it a funeral. You'd think Three Ravens was President of the United States the way they treated him after that, which only made things worse. Should'a rolled the corpse in the river down the east side of the pyramid same as every other victim. Oh no, instead it had a palanquin and flowers and virgin maidens and a feathered headdress, all for this bloke with a hole in his chest the size of bowling ball.

"This is the stone, the very one as destroyed the greatest Indian empire west of the Iroquois. They who could have held off the pioneers from ever crossing the Mississippi and had they not panicked, there'd be buffalo yet in Kansas. Because of this stone, this very stone, none of that happened."

Uncle Henry sat quietly on the stool, rolling the stone in his hands. On it was a terrible scar.

Three Ravens

Two Grey Stones

Every Christmas, my uncles, who were semi-professional liars, told their stories. These great misshapen uncles, who had been most of everywhere, or so they said; been to the Klondike, and survived the Little Big Horn, supped with Custer himself the night before, and hunted rabbits with Buffalo Bill. When we heard this it was rather confounding because we thought Mister Cody was bison specific, only to learn there were seasons when the buffalo were not found and it was either rabbit or else.

As a child, I had about me a geological deposit of uncles who were a vast raw ore, vast as the Mesabi; uncles who been to the Congo, sailed the Horn in the Cutty Sark, shrunk heads in Borneo, and had an artifact to prove it . . . a rock to tell the story by. Every Christmas these uncles wound themselves in their story robes and set fire to our hearts as we listened in earnest fervor.

There was the story of a bear hunt in Minnesota as had the gall stone to prove it. We learned a close ancestor had killed the Lanark dragon as resided in one of the crueler realms of Scotland about a thousand years previous, none other than Angus, son of Bean, who even so long ago resembled our family; small, wiry and full of freckles, he who put an end to the dragon who was disturbing the peace, and did so without bloodshed or endangering the species.

Stories and stones, uncles told, that went back to the Aztecs and Montezuma by way of our long past cousin, O'Reilly, captured by the Spanish, fitted with an iron collar and a length of number seven chain, and ended up with Cortez for being glib in Gaelic as was thought a fair equal to whatever the heathens were saying. How cousin O'Reilly had a scam going with Mister Montezuma as would have saved Mexico 'cepting Montezuma muffed a chip shot and a thousand years of decent empire caved in. All this being true and gospel because there was the stone to prove it, an adobe brick speckled of the virgin's blood sacrificed to the sake of the corn; like what kid with a hoe could fail to identify with that?

We had a meteorite found in the Mongolian desert by Uncle Tamus on his way to Tibet after the Crimean War which he, coincidentally as you might guess, also narrowly escaped. How the meteorite saved his life, for the Mongols who are cruel enough in ordinary circumstance, woulda eaten him for an appetizer save this curious, convoluted, molten-looking rock found in the middle of the waste where not another is found. Not another in a thousand miles give or take, and how them Mongols had never seen such a stone before, the desert being such a powerful bunch of sand, and along comes Uncle Tamus who they just as soon eat as look at, in his pocket a blistered-up, bubbly stone, black as night and feeling sorta strange and heavy in the hand. Glib Uncle Tamus telling how it fell from the sky, as is remarkable, was made of nickel mostly, and started out in the asteroid belt between here and Mars, none of which they knew before, neither about Jupiter or Saturn or Neptune, as a result they kept him alive. And it was afterward we listened better to the teacher during science class, knowing English grammar and mathematics would not have saved speckled Uncle Tamus, but an ear for science surely did.

When it came to Christmas stories, my family was well-supplied. The standard tale about some Mid-East guy paying his taxes, whose wife had been unfaithful, who didn't practice safe sex besides, how a silver-spoon kid was born in a feedbox, seemed by comparison plain and lackluster, with or without the angels. I had uncles who took it as a point of honor to tell a story as was one full peck better than every other uncle's story, and I had heaps of uncles. I had great uncles, great great uncles, uncles-in-law, weird uncles from Chicago and mountain man uncles from LaCrosse who told stories that could make your bladder squirm. The only rule being every story must have a stone.

Like said, I was early on ruined for the regulation Christmas story, so ruined in fact I felt sorry for the New Testament as weren't half the measure to what my uncles provoked in the warm tidepool of a green tree. It was obvious to me that the point of the Christmas story, of Christmas itself, was to render what is ordinary into something else. To transform the resident humbug dwelling in the human heart, and this why every year my uncles, my dottering wrecked uncles, wound their way to the story seat, and there unfurled from their pockets, their handkerchiefs, shop rags and tissue paper, the stone and its telling. Every Christmas it had been so, for a thousand years give or take. All them stones, all them uncles.

And then it was Aunt Millie's turn.

It wasn't that females were not allowed to tell stories, it's just that they didn't. Why this was so I can't say. It was as if the stone wasn't a thing the female could do. After all, some of the stories told by my uncles weren't very nice, some ended badly. How it was sometimes the bad guys won, and the resident boast about the triumph of righteousness is not how it always happens.

Which did not prevent Aunt Millie from wanting her chance. Did I say how we called her Auntie Milliped from the way she scurried, like a thing found under a damp log? Aunt Millie was not the kind of female as is denied, despite no female had, in the last thousand years, been allowed to tell the stone. We all knew what kind of a story she was going to tell, something female, something gushy, mushy and rose-scented. Still, it was only fair she had the chance; even if it was gonna be insufferable, we'd just have to sit still for it. After all, it was Christmas. And 'cause Aunt Millie might take out a length of our skull with her walking stick, a smart length of hornbeam she carried on account of her hip, by which she could knock the eyebrow off a gnat. Aunt Millie wasn't the kind you messed with, and this why she was allowed to take the story seat, arrange a cushion on it and commence:

"I was born in 1882 in Nebraska, a year after my parents, Roland and Julia, entered that godforsaken region. To say Nebraska is empty is to overstate the evidence. Nebraska was not only empty, it was hollow, and the only worse thing is a cold hollow, and that Nebraska could do as well. From the homestead you could walk in a straight line for a week and in that time see nothing the least different from where you started. Where other places had hills and marshes, Nebraska had none. Nebraska was one unrelieved horizon after another, each exactly the same as the previous.

"My father raised corn; field corn, indian corn, popcorn, yellow corn, white corn, purple corn and black corn. The corn was fed to chickens and pigs. Mama kept a garden and that is how we lived. In the fall we'd butcher the animals and father'd disappear over the horizon for a week, returning with a wagonful of supplies; a sheet metal stove, window glass, bolts of cloth, books, candlewicking and kerosene. Right behind him, winter arrived.

"Winter in Nebraska is variable; some years it rained, not regular rain as happens in other places. In Nebraska it rained mud, mud from the outset which is the only way of explaining how the mud got so deep. Some years it snowed, two feet at a time wasn't unusual, sometimes right over the mud. Other years the wind turned hard out of the north and blew and blew and didn't quit for three months straight.

"Father raised corn, each year a few more acres. He started with two but by the time I was big enough to help, it was forty acres of corn. Every year there was planting, weeding and harvest. Early I learned the necessary art of the corn hook. A kind of leather harness worn on the working hand with a slender hook attached used to shuck corn from the stalk, and in turn throw an ear into the air to ricochet off the bang board on the wagon. After a bit of practice, I could shuck blindfolded, throw the cob without looking and bang it home every time. I remember how we'd each take a row and follow it the length of the field as the horses kept pace, three or four rows to the side of the wagon being shucked at a single pass, the corn soaring through the air and hitting the bang board. It was not a musical sound.

"As the field increased in size, so the problem of harvesting the corn as quickly as possible lest it be lost to an early blizzard or the mud. This when father hired Deuteronomy Joe, who was Omaha. When he worked out fine the first year, he was hired again the next. Soon Deuteronomy Joe was a fixture and father built him a nice shack out behind the corn cribs; had a stove, a window, a table, two chairs, and a bed, though we all used the same outhouse.

"Deuteronomy was a Lutheran Indian as is the best kind; the Methodist Indians kept reverting to the bottle and the Catholic ones never let go of it. He was thirty or so when he first came to us and lived another thirty-five after. Tall, lean, did I say he was Omaha, missing some teeth so his face collapsed around his lower jaw, eyes dark as postholes. When he grinned his face became almost grotesque, resembling one of those varmints on the rain gutters of French cathedrals. Deuteronomy Joe tended the horses, hoed the garden, snared the rabbits, and could shuck corn faster than any human ever. He took three rows to one of ours and kept the pace all day. When the first corn picker appeared in 1917, a single row contraption pulled by a tractor on an offset hitch, the dealer offered a free machine to any farmer who could out-shuck this engine across an 80 rod row, notwithstanding the machine was pulled by a tractor. Father entered Deuteronomy Joe in the contest, as neighboring farmers did enter their own hands or themselves against the machine. Biggest event of the season in Wheeler County it was. The crowd was thought near a thousand, which is pretty close to a million when you figure these people came from a place where you can't see another person on the horizon. There were some twenty contestants who thought they could out-shuck the mechanical, but after the first man lost by twenty rods, there weren't many who still felt that way.

"Lordy sakes, did that machine make blazes at shucking corn, spitting each cob off the stalk over a pair of revolving cylinders, cob went off all kitty funkle, while the stalk got sucked underneath the contraption. Faster than you could blink it happened.

"Only two contestants remained who thought they might still best the soon-to-be famous Wood Brothers corn picker. The first lost by only a hundred paces, as weren't bad considering; the other was our Deuteronomy Joe who had yet to try. The crowd had started to wander off figuring this wasn't gonna be even close since none of the others had been, and this last fellow appeared to be an injun, and most of them were Catholic where they used real wine at the communion table, and according to Methodists, how sometimes the bread didn't even get passed.

"The implement dealer started to pull off the field when my father told him another contestant was ready to try. The man laughed in a demeaning way, saying how the price of parafin oil was hardly worth the expense of going across the field again. Then he went on to say, '*It is plain as day no living person can beat a corn picker powered by a 12 horse engine.*

"' *So who's the fool?*' the implement dealer said in a voice way over-loud. '*Who's yet the fool who thinks to out-shuck this machine? Who Roland? You?*'

"'*Neep,*' that's how my father said no. '*Neep, ain't me, but my hired man Joseph,*' at which point he put his arm around the shoulder of Deuteronomy.

"'*Don't tell me Roland Carpenter . . . you intend to race my machine with . . . an injun?*' questioned the implement dealer."

Aunt Millie interjected, "That was my name before I married into grandfather's family.

"The implement dealer continued, '*You're daft. I ain't wasting my machine, my tractor or my fuel oil against any fool Indian.*'

"At which point father extracted from his pocket a $50 gold piece. The implement dealer swallowed real hard at the sight of it.

"'*Well neighbor, your coin is as good as gone, but you've got yourself a race.*'

"'*Now just hold a minute,*' said my dad, '*just a damn minute. I ain't much into the customs of the gambling vice, but it seems to me if I raise the stake, you're obligated to do likewise.*'

"The implement dealer, who knew very well a

raised ante when he saw one, who had come all the way from Omaha and was a little peeved, but for an easy fifty dollars in gold said, *'If your toothless wonder beats my machine, the corn picker is yours and I'll throw in the tractor.'"* It was a McCormick-Deering. He shouldna done that.

"You can already guess how the story ends, how Deuteronomy Joe out-shucked the Wood Brothers mechanical and beat it hands down by twenty paces, and how my father got his first tractor and corn picker, though we didn't use the thing for a year after that 'cause we didn't have the fuel. How after the war with corn prices good and soon everybody had a tractor.

"Deuteronomy Joe lived out his life in the shack behind the cribs. Did I say it had a little kitchen and bedroom, with a corn shuck mattress same as everybody else and a cob roof for storing cob to burn in the cob stove? The corn cob stove was how we kept the winter at bay in Nebraska. My mama had one, Deuteronomy Joe had one, everybody in the big nowhere of Nebraska had a cob stove. Had a little bitty fire chamber about the size of a rural route mailbox, cast iron grate and a tube with an external lip that was loaded with cobs just like a breech shotgun. A plunger injected the cobs into the firebox, actually it was more like a damp fuse they burned.

"In the kitchen was a large box, in the parlor room another, in the dining room a third, a corncob box same as other places had a woodbox. Each attending a stove and that's how we wintered. The morning chore being to fill the cob box, fire the stove with a bit of paper till the cobs themselves started. They didn't burn openly like wood but stumbled along more like charcoal. We had lots of cobs. Mountains of them. My father like everyone else took his corn to market as grain, after running the cob through a sheller powered by a Fairbanks & Morse, one cob at a time, forty acres worth.

"Christmas in Nebraska was like Christmas everywhere. We'd gaze at the Sears and Roebuck catalog wishing for this and every other thing. The week before Christmas father made the trip to Omaha by horse and returned with what he could afford. A doll for me, some bath water for Mama, a corkgun for my brother, and that was Christmas, but not the one that burns in my mind as if it were yesterday.

"In Nebraska, you see, we had no trees. Lilacs grew hesitantly along the road where father planted them. In the bottoms where streams ran in the spring there was a kind of alder. Otherwise there were no trees and you can not very well keep Christmas without a tree, can you? Or at least something that looks like a tree. My parents were not idle savages when it came to Christmas, so of course we must have a tree, at least a thing in the general direction of a tree. This why we fashioned in the middle of the parlor an enormuos cornshock. Everybody had seen cornshocks and noticed how they resembled Indian tepees, and if you are desperate, and in Nebraska, Christmas trees. So it was we had in our parlor this enormous, fantastic corn tree whose tassle was folded over by the ceiling. A fine tree it was, resembling in the lamp light a pyramid of the fine beaten gold.

"To this cornshock we tied all manner of ribbons, candy canes, feathers, arrowheads. I remember a tiny brass bell, garlands of popcorn, we had lots of popcorn. We did not put candles on our tree lest the house burn down.

"Being a proper if oversized cornshock, it was of consequence hollow on the inside, a most hallowed place, and it was in this tiny chancel father sat on a braided rug each and every Christmas Eve and read the story according to St. Luke.

"Then my mother would sit there and read O'Henry, sometimes Dickens, sometimes Zane Grey.

"I remember when winter arrived, Deuteronomy spent the evening meal with us, and likewise at Christmas. Each year father gave him a new pipe, a hat, and a pair of shoes. I remember the year father gave him a child's coloring book and crayons and how he was very delighted. Each year he listened to the stories from the cornshock, quiet as was his way. Then one year and quite out of character, he asked if he too could tell a story.

"So Deuteronomy Joe sat on the braided rug, crossed his legs "indian fashion" and from his pocket withdrew two stones. The first was a small, rather boat-shaped stone, though I have come to think since it more resembles a cradle." At this point Aunt Millie who, if you've forgotten, was telling the story, withdrew from her purse a small, oddly-shaped stone.

"*'In the beginning,'* Deuteronomy said, *'the Great Spirit did fashion the world. It was wide and vast, filled with all manner of stars and mountains, rivers, skies and clouds, but it was a sad place despite all this beauty . . . for it was empty of living things. So empty you could feel it. Like a canoe without a paddle, a cradle without a blanket, a sky without a bird, a river without a trout, a song without words. For even the Great Spirit, without a people, is not very great.*

" *'So it was the Great Mystery gave the earth its birds, its trees, its fishes, and filled the terrible emptiness with life.'*

"Deuteronomy placed in the hollow of the first stone, a second small round stone and said,*'The Great Spirit knew what he had done, that life, feeble as it was, was as great as the world and the planets and the stars and all the heavens. This the Great Spirit did not know before.*

" *'And when the Great Spirit grew sad that the tribes did war on one another, and burned his prairies, and killed all the buffalo, he picked up the one small stone with the hollow upon it and then the round stone, and placing them together, looked on them and thought better of vengeance.'* "

Then Aunt Millie was done. Her story ended. In one hand she held the hollow stone and in the other the round stone, and when she placed them together, they did kinda fit one with the other. We passed them around, touching the same stones Deuteronomy Joe had touched, same as were touched by a hundred generations of Omaha a thousand years before Columbus. Same exact stones.

Two Grey Stones

Adah's Turn

Sexual liberation had arrived the Christmas before when Millie, the sister-in-law, was the first woman in history to tell a stone story. Not once in the preceding thousand years had this happened and now it was about to happen two years in a row. Uncle Ed still had his fur up 'cause Millie had taken the seat, and because the story she told was a lot better than he believed, well . . . a woman was capable of. Now Adah wanted her turn; god in pajamas, what was the world coming to? "This no ordinary stone is," the obligatory first line, and she got it right.

That George had married Adah in 1898 was a surprise. At 27 years he was thought a little long of tooth, and distractable, an untamed kind, meaning a farmer, not the kind to marry a woman like Adah, who was considered well-traveled, for she had been to Fond du Lac on the train, also Wausau. For a farmer to marry the school marm was routine enough, in fact had proven itself the essential method to foist onto the goodness of manhood those plain, tall and slender female folk who might not otherwise enjoy the indignities of genetic replication. Adah didn't need the help of any farmer to get herself married off, she could have had her choice in the village and a big house with a sleep-in-maid. Was said of Adah she had a length of wild weed in her, and very near a Catholic; if that didn't set the tongues flapping. A Roman, a papist, in the family of them Wesleyan kind, surprise be if their blood didn't coagulate.

That George had nearly married a Catholic was averted when Adah's father, also named George, finding no church of that stripe on the Wisconsin frontier, switched over to Episcopalian as close enough approximation. A catechism for which heads had rolled in the realm of Elizabeth. What converted Adah's father was a woods separate and deep enough to dim God, the church was at best a distant muffled thud. Not that George Tragasser cared particularly, the only services he required of the kirk were those simple observations of birth, marriage and death. Over these entrances and departures the church might have its say, of all other things between, the kirk could take its chances like everything else.

Still it was a reach that George, the suitor, had married Adah, the Espicopalian, when the family with some personal effort had thrown off the heavy mantle of that aristocratic synod. They having been hymn blowers now for three generations, a grandfather baptized by John Wesley himself in 1779, that being the son of James who was also the son of James. This the family custom, to name the first born son as James, in honor of the version. The King James Version, this James the I, the former Scot, son of Queen Mary of the same, who was certified non-Catholic and thought well of witchcraft. This terrible pattern of naming, once established, took on a contagious aspect to the succeeding generations. With it, a fearful sense of breaking any presumed luck the family might possess should they dare change a thing so basic as always naming the first born son James, when it had been so for most always. A kind of witchcraft it was, if it did render cemeteries a wee dull to have them fill with the same name, generation after generation. Giving to any observer the sense of pernicious decay, of life controlled by the grave, and one's life but a fleeting episode before it too would join the throng of James piling up in the kirkyard.

It was this sort of drear spell that caused James the 10th, maybe the 20th, to emigrate to Boston in 1842, in a flight not from tyranny and oppression but the swelling presence of that boneyard. In 1852 he did establish on a dirt road a little below the village of Rushville, as was in turn below Algernon and Springville and Whiting, they a little separated from Middleton; all of them mill towns, the choice being grist or lumber with the occasional shingle mill thrown in for binder. There was James in 1852, minding his hostel catering to the teamsters as worked the freight between Stevens Point and Big Bull Falls, also Little Bull and the more distant centers of commerce of New Berlin and Fremont. Providence was his trade, hay for horses, supper and board for the leather-throated teamsters, all for a shingle a night, as a shilling was then called in the Pinery, a square of shingles was worth about a shilling wholesale. As it happened, James was not above taking trade for accomodation, particularly at wholesale. A smoked ham was worth a week's lodging and could get the horses a pail of oats besides. Trout, fresh and cleaned, wss worth a fried ham supper for two with dance music provided by black man Lew, with two mugs of homebrew in the timber room, what they called the tavern. The timber room because the bar itself was constituted of one entire pine log, hewn down till what remained of it stood four foot high and three across, whose surface was jackplaned till it glowed, it being dumped over with a mixture of beeswax and bear oil that so permeated the wood that twenty years after when it was replaced by a standard barroom font, it still smelled of bear.

That Adah was nearly Catholic might have ruined any chance of her marrying George, but she was coincidentally the granddaughter of Charlie, this Charlie Rice, in these parts endorsement enough. For the Rice hotel had been far known and famous, owing it was here in the time before . . . before statehood, before the settlers, before the lumber barrons, before the place was chewed up and rendered hospitable by that ceaseless swarm.

"This no ordinary stone is," said Adah. That we could see . . . plainly it was no ordinary stone. In fact it was not stone, but brick. Not at all what stone stories are supposed to be. Uncle Ed was already shaking his head; didn't he say stone stories are not for females to do! They are not bricks, but stones, honest kinds of stones, stone stories, real stories that cause a dampness under the arms and maybe even squeeze your knees together if done right. Not about bricks.

We all could see, Adah was going to blow her chance. Not that females don't know stories, they just tend to leave out the good stuff, the gore. Females leave out the gore. They might tell a story about a dragon but will include a napkin, and a prayer before the meal. A female will describe the scene but it will be decorative, even if it's a cave.

Guys do not commit this kind of sin against a story, though they will describe, and intricately, how a dragon's teeth are arranged in the jaw bone so when the mandible closes down on a victim the teeth intersect with a final and audible suddenness severing the vital organs in a wholesale sort of way resulting in an enormous blood loss, in the instant rendering the victim unconscious to the actual chewing . . . this where females generally leave off. A female does not proceed with the same details, the sound of the blood dripping on the floor and how the dragon with a long purple tongue licked up the pool and the red mud altogether. So a kid does not remember female stories the same way. Because females detour around the most salient observations, and as a consequence leave the image unresolved. As can bother a kid in the middle and particularly dark latitudes of the night. When the same story, in the fierce rendition of an uncle, the same dragon, the same bad end, but carries through honestly and describes death by dragon as altogether similar to getting killed by a sawmill, and surprisingly painless. Same as when a white shark bites off your bottom half, you ain't gonna hang around screaming like it says in the movies 'cause your hydraulic pressure is gone and so are you. Which is comforting to a kid in an odd sort of way during the darker part of night.

So where did dear old Adah think she could take a story about a brick? Borrrrrrring. Maybe we ought just ask her to let one of the uncles have the chair?

She began with, "For it is this brick of the great lum of Charlie Rice, Town of Plover, 1842. Not that Charlie Rice was ever famous but his chimney was, for in 1842 an inn house with a brick chimney was not just a rare thing, it was spectacular. For in those days, the domain north of the Winnebago was odious woods, a limitless and undiminished woods, an unblemished woods. The same woods Charlie Rice bethought did hold his livelihood if not his fortune and his child's also. An enterprising sort might attempt to gain a living as a woodsman but that would mean an axe, a saw pit, and when this is done, ride the crib of new-sawn out on the spring freshet.

"Charlie Rice was lazier than that. He could have set up a trading post the like of John Baptiste DuBay, but the commerce with Indians was diminishing, and besides, Charlie Rice was lazier than that. He might have farmed, though the region was a bit northward for wheat, only rye grew here with any enthusiasm and bread rendered of rye flour is like mortar cement. Corn was chancey and not directly transportable, if converted to smoked hams required a herdsman who would keep the pigs from wolf, fox and black bear. Charlie Rice was lazier than that. The wonder is why Charlie came to the big woods in the first place.

"He knew the trail they'd follow. He knew where to get in their way. If he could insert the crudest resource of hospitality between the foot-and-forest-weary traveler and their destination, he could invoke the penny from the most reluctant, that they might spend a night away from the forest, take their comfort, sleep in a real bed, eat from a real plate, use a spoon, also a fork and knife, on real roast beef with boiled carrots and taties and neeps. And he, Charlie, might charge the poor delirious pilgrim two shillings for the favor. Charlie Rice was exactly that lazy.

"In 1843 Charlies built a "hotel" on the bank of the Wisconsin River just below where the Little Plover adds in, a pompous, two story colonial with white clapboard siding as was not only rare in the woods, it was like finding a circus tent pitched in an Indian village or that some wandering stone age savages had thrown up like the Notre Dame complete with stained glass windows and staring gargoyles. Charlie's hotel was so much more than unususal, it was a freak. And most audacious of all, what made Charlie Rice's hotel splendorous wasn't white clap or the sandstone foundation, nor the beer tun beneath the kitchen floor . . . what made it a mirage to the journeyman who had not seen civilized habitation since Kenosha and the Arlington Prairie; what made the Rice hotel the place to stop between Ft. Howard and Trempeleau, between Portage and Jenny Bull Falls was it had a brick chimney, a red brick chimney two and a half stories high, wide across as a laid-out corpse with his shoes and socks on." Not a bad simile for a female-told story. "A brick chimney in the middle of a wilderness nowhere, none else like it between the North pole and the North star, all two and a half stories of it.

"By that chimney, smack in the middle of the widest forest ever witnessed of humankind, a woods as ran from Fort Fremont to Chequamegon, a godbillion board foot of white-assed pine and dear Charlie's brick lummin' chimney smack in the middle.

"Everybody knew that Charlie Rice, my grandfather, made his fortune in a time too short to be entirely legal. Two shillings a night for fried ham and a blanketed bed was an outrageous overcharge, 'ceptin' for the proximity of the brick chimney. Like said, smack in the middle of nowhere. Staying at the Rice Hotel was like having a supper with Queen Victoria, who was homely enough but not yet the same as a brick chimney, two and a half stories of brick, on a hostile October night in a woods deeper that the devil's own cellar. It was nearly criminal and a little unChristian of him, to have an edifice set before the traveler who was ever so weary of the woods, in a way we can not now imagine. For whom two shillings a night was not only a bargain, it was cheap therapy.

"In ten years time Charlie made his fortune. The hotel was sold, soon after caught fire and burned to the ground, the bricks duely scattered, all two and a half stories of them, save this one."

At that, Adah quit talking.

Adah's Turn

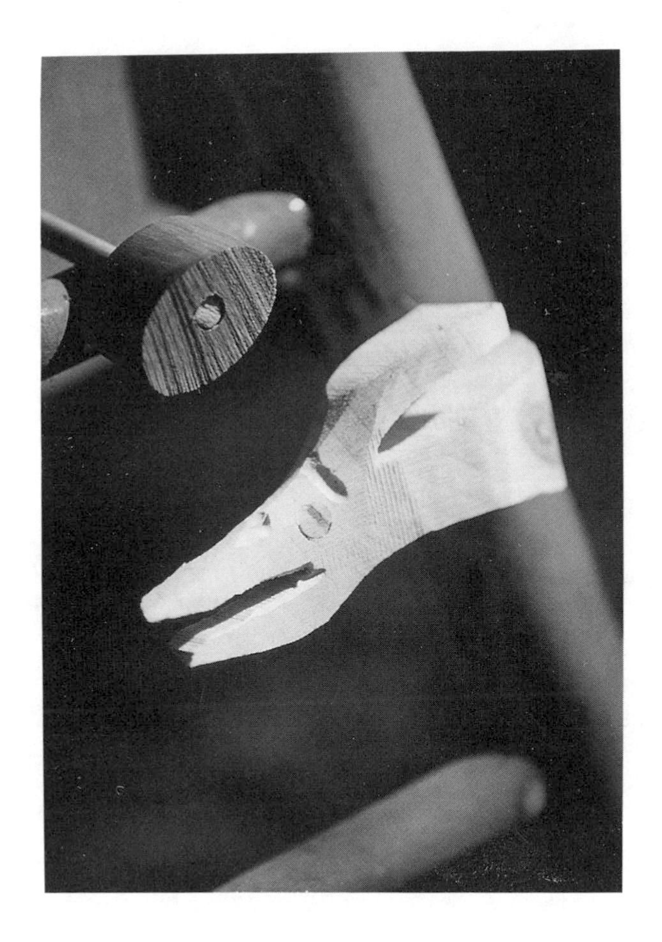

The Eye of the Wolf

Heavily. Uncle Ed, The Gaunt, sat down. The chair whinnied. He less sat than crash-landed.

He was called The Gaunt for he was thin. Very near hollow was Uncle Ed. He looked chewed. We all knew Uncle Ed was gonna die at any time, which is why we sat at a distance in case he went over; we didn't want to be in his way, he was that overdue.

Uncle Ed slowly uncoiled his hand. Actually, less a hand than a claw, and it not very high grade. Gnarled weren't the word for it, not by half. Gnarled were his hands, gnarled as the worst limb on a black oak tree. A fenceline black oak at that, with barbwire and staples driven in and grown over, a broken, wind-spent, horse-bit, collision kind of tree . . . these the hands of Uncle Ed. He didn't open his hands exactly. They reluctantly uncoiled, at least part way. In his palm, a stone.

"This no ordinary stone is," croaked Uncle Ed. Then, he snorted and kind of hiccuped and a vengeful light shone in his blood-shot eyes. "Not a stone at all is it," whispered Uncle Ed, leaner than a malnourished toothpick. "No ordinary stone is this," he hissed in a voice as fragile as a bone china teacup. "No stone," sighed The Gaunt who we thought so near dead he should keep nickels in his front pocket and a cork in his back, as is pretty near . . . dead.

We thought maybe Uncle Ed should skip his turn being it is hard for him to breathe much less tell a story full length. Like said, 'cause he might drop plumb dead right before our eyes, as could spoil Christmas. But only sorta since he was so overdue.

"A wolf eye is this," he said, though it was more snarled. "This is ney stane, but a wolf eye. I remember wolves."

In his hand was a stone, least it was hard like a stone, 'course so was Uncle Ed. A stone as did resemble an eye. A blue eye with a dark, black pupil that mighta been an eye . . . once. The resemblence was close. Coulda been an eye. Mighta been. Uncle Ed was far too old to lie, being that he might die at any minute and that last untruth coming at a critical moment, sending him to hell forever and ever, so it stood to reason Uncle Ed wouldn't lie 'cause he might not live to see the next comma, much less correct the error in the text.

The stone did glisten like an eye. Uncle Ed wouldn't lie, not with his soul so close to the hole. A good man wouldn't take the risk.

"I remember wolves, remember when they were common, if not quite numerous. Every night beyond the village you could hear their lonesome. That what it were,not a howl but a lonesome. It is one thing to hear a wolf howl in the broad daylight, it is another thing to hear the howl after dark against the night. The place of a sudden bigger, wider, and all of it owned by the wolf.

"I remember P.J. Barnsdale, Frankie's great uncle, trapped wolves. Frankie Barnsdale being the clerk at the feedmill and midget; he once worked in a circus, afterwards the clerk at the feedmill. Bounty being a dollar each, he and Indian Peck done a business trapping and shooting wolves on the long hill. County Clerk didn't want them to bring in the pelt, just the head caped out, this to get the dollar each. Punched holes in the ears to mark the scalp so smart-alecks didn't bring in the same fur a week later. Coulda been a dog scalp I suppose, but not likely 'cause the dog might have an owner as could shoot back.

"I remember a wolf, and his name was Wiggy and he lived on the east-west road long before it got a name in the platbook. Old Man Wiggy, we called him, 'cause he was old and weird. I remember the black overalls he wore. His hair came to his shoulders, cruel black hair he had. His face like Moses, stony, coulda been a mobster with that look . . . heavy eyelids, mighta been Italian.

"Teddy and Joe lived on the southeast corner of Section 2, Township 22 North, Range 8 East. The farm, a square parcel of a hundred and sixty acres. A small but tidy house, several out-sheds, a plain rafted barn, milk-house, in the middle of the biggins the granary and tool-close. The front door of the house faced the town road and, as custom, rarely used. Directly across the road was the bruised profile of a crabapple tree. Situated that farm boys intent on stealing apples had first to settle their conscience enough to steal apples before the front stoop of crazy Teddy. They could then proceed with the bellyache. West of the house spilled a benevolent clump of lilacs that when combined with May did submerge the eastern half of the township in outrageous purple verse.

"Joe Wiggy was a passable farmer and a better mechanic; he kept cows but later sold the herd and worked at odd jobs of mechanical repair. The Wiggys came to the town mysteriously; they had no relatives in the area, which in this township is mystery enough. Was in 1936 they moved to Section 2, rumor had it they came from New York; actually it was Chicago.

"Teddy had once been married, a socialite. You know the type." Actually we didn't. "Willowy, bobbed hair, slinky dress. Her family had money, I mean lots. She was supposed to have been beautiful.

"Was an accident, a motorcar accident, Ted crushed in the car, she thrown out and killed. The car was something you probably never will see in these parts, a Model J Duesenberg, four-passenger phaeton. That's what they called them then." Nice word isn't it? . . . phaeton.

"The Wiggys originally came from Philadelphia, the family well-to-do. As a student in France, Theodore studied literature and music; coincidentally he fell in love with automobiles, one in particular, the Type 35 Bugatti. They were French cars that used castor oil instead of petroleum for a lubricant. Castor oil rendered from skunks and certain other burrow animals, which only the French would think of. His family thought he was at the Sorbonne when he was elbow-deep in the nickel-plated straight-eight, two-liter with double overhead camshaft on needle bearings. Teddy had no difficulty getting a job at the Bugatti factory due to his musical ear, able to cue the difference of a connecting rod over-torqued. When he returned to the States, Teddy searched out Fred Duesenberg and handed him a note signed by the famous Ettore Bugatti and was hired on the spot; his job to deliver new cars and as part of the price, teach customers the intricacies of a Duesenberg; the maintenance, lubrication and skills of high speed driving.

"Teddy was an impressive agent for Deusenberg. He swore in French, played a Chopin sonata, a Stauss Waltz, he would bow when a lady entered, recite a toast to Robert Bruce in the Gaelic or the balcony scene from Romeo and Juliet in Elizabeth's English.

"She was a customer's daughter and they had only been married three years when the truck sideswiped them, Teddy not altogether blameless. The car had been traveling one hundred and six miles an hour and it was two thirty in the morning. He had driven faster. Besides delivering cars, Duesenberg had him run-in the engine and frame for five hundred miles at the Indianapolis race-track before the coach body was fitted. A bare frame, engine, drive train and a seat wired to the frame, and a fool brave enough to hang on. The open frame J-Type Duesenberg was capable of a hundred and forty miles an hour on eight cylinders and two hundred and sixty-five horsepower. The SJ Model managed one hundred and seventy-five miles an hour with a centrifugal supercharger and three hundred and twenty horsepower.

"Teddy suffered a broken skull, fractured ribs,

blurred vision and slurred speech. In time his vision returned, his speech never quite, when he spoke French it hardly seemed to matter. The woman was buried in the family plot before he regained consciousness.

"Soon after, Joe bought the farm in central Wisconsin. Priced at two dollars and seventy cents an acre, the improvements another eleven hundred dollars. Joe always wanted to live in the country; something dependable about country. It was 1936 and a man could use something dependable, especially a man with a broken brother who woke in the night singing French songs.

"Joe's hope was Teddy would get better away from the city, away from long-nosed automobiles that might remind him of her. At times Teddy was lucid, he'd look over some broken machine and offer a few words about bearing wobble. Then there were nights when Teddy recited poetry, in god knows what language. He fashioned poems about how Bugattis look like frogs, how they smelled of beavers. Joe doubted Teddy would ever be well again.

"It doesn't take long for a neighborhood to notice strangeness. When Joe and Ted Wiggy arrived, Joe immediately fit in because of his mechanical skills, he was also a passable blacksmith. Teddy was strange. He kept to himself, he spoke a language ever so much worse than Polish, he gazed at things in a remote way. His hair was long, like Buffalo Bill's. Like Custer's. He kept to himself and everbody was happy with the arrangement, including the crabapple out in the front of their place, that in the fall actually had apples on it.

"Wolves were thought extinct from these parts with

the assistance of P.J. Barnesdale and Indian Peck; a dollar each didn't help their cause. The last had its hide hung to the lumber shed behind the village hardware for six months in 1902. Few believed a wolf was roaming the Buena Vista Marsh in 1937. Some claimed to have seen tracks, heard a howl, a howl even to those uneducated knew in their bones was that mystical creature. The marsh had coyotes, most had heard the coyote and its yawning sort of note; it was not the same.

"The wolf howl was different, the very earth seemed to transmit the vibration. In the dark the sound could raise the hair on the back of a person's neck, hair most people forgot had erectile muscle attached. Farmers worried about the cattle and young stock, and wanted to blow a hole in whatever it was as could give such a noise. It was, they thought, an indecent sound for a settled country, some took to carrying rifles to their fields. There were arguments at the feedmill over who had actually seen, who shot at what, and certain families no longer sat in the same pew on the same side of church. Their farm dog had turned up missing and a familiar-looking hide was nailed to a neighbor's barn door. This, on the rumor of a wolf.

"A wolf track is the size of a large fist."

Uncle Ed, who is telling the story, tried to form a fist to show us how big a print was the wolf. His hand closed in such slow motion he gave up on the demonstration and resumed. Oddly he didn't seem half so dead as when he started talking.

"There were kids, adventurous kids, who took to the idea of making plaster-of-paris casts of the wolf print. They pestered their mothers to let them sleep outdoors so they could hear it, and when they did, came running to the house breathless, unable to talk. There were mothers whose mistake was thinking the effect was fear.

"The neighborhood talked of a collection to hire up a government hunter. The wolf might attack cattle, surely ruin the deer herd, and hadn't they read of wolves killing colts and children? With winter coming, and winter makes everything meaner, it would be best to settle down fears of the countryside.

"Was about here someone took a shot at Teddy, a thirty-thirty fired at an unusual and, they said, hairy shape seen loping, they said, across the night field. The mistake was immediately noted. Well, he did look wolfish. I mean, what's a man doing out at that time of night? The bullet passed cleanly through Teddy's calf; treated with rubbing alcohol and rags, the wound healed quickly.

"But it provoked something in Teddy, he felt the more related to the creature. Joe warned him, *'Next time they won't miss, they'll shoot you dead.'* The advice fell without effect. Joe knew his brother well enough to know it was useless to try.

"At the local Community Club the menfolk grumbled about potato prices at fifteen cents a hundred and whether they would ever save enough to buy a tractor. Some believed tractors altogether too complicated and expensive to be useful. They talked of wolf. One said he had a cow to go down with milk fever, how he dragged it to the woods and poisoned the carcass with strychnine. He was sure to get the thing. *'I slit the belly open and hung the guts from a tree for the wind to better catch the scent.'*

"This aroused some contrary opinion. *'Yah damn fool, you'll kill every farm dog, cat and runaway pig for twenty miles around with that stunt. Besides, a wolf won't eat carrion unless there is nothing else. My dad once told me the wolf and mankind are related.'* This observation didn't set well with some and they said so.

"*'I tell you an animal is an animal and a man is a man. I ain't related to no mangy wolf.'* He ought not have said the part about being 'related to a bitch.' Soon after, the first punch was thrown.

"The women gathered at the coffee pot knew exactly when the discussion had digressed, for the community hall had gone suddenly quiet. They grabbed the cookie plate and coffee pot and went to loosen things up before another 'discussion' broke out.

"While these dairymen and potato farmers were trying to sing Christmas carols, Teddy sat cross-legged in the SE corner of the NW corner of Section 13, cross-legged and wrapped in a blanket. Sitting on a low sand knoll as rose over the dreary marsh. A west wind drove his scent into the tangle of hemlock and balsam behind him. Before him, lay the flat expanse of what locals called, Old Pete. His eyes came to adjust and despite the darkness he could see a remarkable distance. It was eleven o'clock when Teddy began to howl.

"The sound was one he had heard before, of a supercharged Bugatti at five pounds of boost. Having heard it, you knew it was something powerful, the way it warped and rippled across the land.

"At the community hall the men now calmed moved in a tight circle of chairs and upended stovewood, smoking pipes and handrolls, secretly passing a hip flask. Talking wolf. Peace, it seems, had been restored.

"*'I figure to get the thing before Christmas.'*

"*'Like hell. I just bought a new rifle. A mean looking war surplus, thirty-aught-six. Got a bullet smaller than the thirty-thirty but with a shell case long as my finger. Betcha I get the wolf, 'cause at a mile I can blow the top off a milk can.'*

"*'At a mile?'*

"*'At a mile. Like said, a military rifle. The guy I bought it from said thousands of 'em are stored away somewhere in warehouses.'*

"Was some less than a mile when Teddy first saw the wolf. With the moon he could make out the shadow of it before he could see the creature itself. The wolf followed a deer trail, as he thought it might, for he had been here waiting every night for a week. The animal was smaller than expected, easily confused for a dog. Still, it did not move like a dog. About it was a smoothness, a slippery motion that long ago gave the creature its name, lupus, canis lupus linneaus. Concurrent was the uninvited notion the creature could run forever. Against the darkness and the marsh, the wolf seemed, well, perfected. The unexpected thought touched Teddy. How can a beast be civilized? Hadn't he spent years and other men their fortunes to achieve the same fluidity? That elegance of movement produced only by intelligence and civilization? The Duesenberg used copper-lined hypods filled with mercury to soothe the jerk of the 150 pound crankshaft. The wolf moved like the Deusenberg, it flowed more that it ran, with the airiness, the refinement, the acuity that can be only the product of mastered skills. For the automobile it was gauges; ammeter, oil pressure, fuel, water temperature, revolution counter, chronograph, 150 mph speedometer, altimeter, barometer, brake pressure and a signal box to indicate when it was time to change the oil, check the battery and that the self-lubrication reservoir was empty. The wolf had its perfected sensibilities; its own civilization; that sense of smell, sight, strength of shoulder, power of jaw, and that slippery elegance. Unlike his neighbors, most who thought Charles Darwin was born of cloven hoof, Teddy knew of evolution and believed, sixty million years before, men and wolves were the same family, both cursorial carnivores. Together, man and wolf gained the canine tooth and a sense of wanderlust. Wolves live in packs, they cooperate, they hunt together. Wolf pups must be taught to hunt and to share, rather like Sunday School. Sometimes wolves leave territory to let the game build up again, just like farmers fallow land. They scent-mark their territory to warn away strangers, same as men use bagpipes and flags. They map their domains with scented roads so to never get lost, bachelor wolves share in the child rearing, and the pups play catch with bones and are scolded for disobedience, and the pack sometimes lets its population grow beyond the food-supply. Sometimes they kill to excess, kill each other, commit suicide. Sometimes they climb trees, howl just to hear themselves howl, and howl because they are in love. The Indian, Teddy read, believed the wolf was holy because it is man's brother.

"'Next time I'll kill them both. I swear, I will kill them both. I mean I had that damn yellow-eyed devil in

my sights when old man Wiggy lets out this howl that turns the wolf away, running off like a fire through a straw barn. I could have tried a couple shots but not with bullets at 25 cents each. That crazy Wiggy. I should've shot him and strung his hide from the barn. Ought to put him away. He's crazy, ya know. And damn if he doesn't look like Karl Marx.'

"Within the week everyone in the neighborhood knew Teddy was a Marxist or a Moslem or a cousin to Mozart, or something pretty rotten. Not that this undercurrent affected how they treated Teddy. In the township it is all right to have feelings but not at all correct to wear them on your sleeve. 'Cause a machine might up and bust and they haulin' it over to Wiggy's to fix, and hadn't they seen Teddy point out something to Joe as if he was telling him how to weld it so they wouldn't have to buy a new one which cost twenty bucks and a whole milk check.

"Maybe Teddy was kinda different and kinda crazy, still he was useful, and weren't they civilized? If a man can't run off with a long piece of twine once in a while they might as well all be shipped to the bubby-hatch. If Teddy wants to spend his nights howling, long as he don't peek in windows or trample down the neighbor's garden or sneak eggs out of the hen house, that then is his own darn what-for.

"Teddy had a nose. Least that's what the French call it. I mean lots of people have noses but Teddy's was special. He could smell the differnce between any two kinds of bread, smoking tobacco or beer. He'd sniff at a crank-case and tell if it was time to change oil. From the living room he knew when Joe was putting too much black pepper on the fried potatoes. Smell is a language all by itself, he'd tell Joe. People smell different, one from the other. You can tell if a man spent the day in the woodlot gathering oak firewood or cutting pine logs for lumber. Whether a woman had been boiling chickens or weeding the garden. If you get close enough, you can tell if she's in love.

"Joe was not really surprised when Teddy disappeared for extended periods, what bothered him was the amounts of water, tea and wine Teddy was consuming. Every time he turned around, Teddy was drinking some fluid. When questioned Teddy simply replied he must be sweating more.

"*'Where do you go anyway? You're up in the small hours, I hear the door close, and you aren't back till mid morning. Last week you were out most of the day. It don't bother me but Teddy, there's people with guns and a few of them bear you personal grievance. In the dark they could shoot you instead of the wolf.'*

"A week later was another discussion between the brothers. *'You mean to tell me you spent seventy-five dollars on that?'*

"*'No, it only cost 32 dollars, the rest was the freight from Manitoba, 43 dollars and fifty cents.'*

"*'Jesus, Ted, why the hell d'yah spend 75 bucks on a dog?'*

"*'It's not a dog, its a Husky.'*

"*'Looks big enough to pull a plow.'*

"*'Joe, don't tell anyone.'*

"*'What?'*

"*'Don't tell about the dog.'*

"*'Why not?'*

"*' Just don't.'* Teddy used a tone of voice peculiar to the species when they come up against something fundamental.

"One rig parked on a lonesome road is bound to attract the second, and the second attract a third. Such is the township's definition of gravity. The first car stopped to borrow a logging chain, the second delivering a box of fudge. The third car stopped 'cause it was Christmas, and they felt like talking. The fourth was afraid he'd slide into the ditch trying to get around the first three. Within the hour three-quarters of the motorcars and half the horses in town were lined up and down the road. Some thought it was a fire, a sawmill accident or something equally memorable.

"The crowd was gathered at the windless side of a barn, looking at a hide nailed to the big sliding door. The man in the center of the crowd was holding his rifle in the cherished pose of supreme weaponry, holding his rifle aloft. As David had held his slingshot, as Arthur his Excaliber, as Sitting Bull his Sharps carbine. Turning a slow circle, grinning, for this was good opera, and for the twelfth time demonstrating how he killed the thing.

"*'Easiest shot I ever made. Was gettin' up stovewood from the lot when I saw it coming. I was real careful to move deliberate so's not to spook it till I got hold of the rifle leaned against a tree. Had it loaded and cocked just in case. Devil never knew what hit him. That, by god, is the last wolf we'll see in this country, a good thing 'cause we can't have beasts like that roaming around the neighborhood. I mean, look at the horrid size of it. And those teeth. Didn't I promise to make a rug out of it? Didn't I? You know, for awhile I wondered. Old Man Wiggy was sneaking around so much I thought he'd spook it. I mean, he's OK you know, but does a sane man howl? I don't know but I think that man has got a bladder problem.'*

"The hide hung on the barn door for six months, nailed in the historic fashion of victims. After awhile people didn't stop any more to gaze on it, the farmer never did make a rug. In June he pulled the hide from the door with a pitch fork and tossed it in a manure spreader. The nails stayed behind, the outline of the hide left an irregular mark on the door till the barn burned in 1951, blamed on a short circuit.

"The farmer did look at the shadow of the spot from time to time, pleasing himself, remembering 1937, the time he had the town road stopped up tighter than a skunk in a stovepipe. How he killed the beast with the first thirty-aught-six in these parts. The distance, with retelling, went from fifty yards to half a mile, then almost a mile, the wind blowing and the wolf running.

"Well, almost a wolf.

"Folks forgot how Theodore Wiggy had been heard howling and rumored with bladder trouble. Some swear on Christmas Eve they can still hear a wolf, or maybe it is Old Man Wiggy howling. How sometimes on a winter night the wind will work itself into a howl, howl at the window, howl across the chimney hole. There are those now who have come to think there is something lovely about a howl."

In the cradle of Uncle Ed's hand lay the stone. It seemed to turn, and like an eye . . . wink.

The Eye of the Wolf

A Christmas of Faith

Ooze. Bernice did ooze. They all said that of Uncle Ed's wife. She might have been described as generous, overflowing or charitable . . . instead the word used on Bernice was ooze. The reason this was so is because Uncle Ed married outside the species, in fact quite a ways beyond the border, a Martian been nearer to us than what was Bernice. She being Polish and Catholic, a Trebatowski, which for my family of befreckled English and blue-painted Scots is twice the reach had Uncle Ed married out of the solar system.

It didn't help that Bernice was educated, she had college degrees in history and math, not a dumb ol' teacher college neither but the University of Cracow and somehow ended up marrying a farmer from central Wisconsin who lived in a house ordered from the Sears and Roebuck catalog and included even the windows and mopboard, all it needed was nails, a hammer and a plumb foundation. Was also said this was how Ed acquired Bernice, from a catalog; maybe it was the other way around.

Was her sisters-in-law who said Bernice oozed, they were envious. In truth they hated Bernice not because she was Polish or Catholic but because she gushed, she bubbled, she boiled, she overflowed. There wasn't anything Bernice couldn't do or figure out. She studied the seed catalog, she bought holstein cows when they were rare, built a silo, raised alfalfa. Uncle Ed had a tractor ten years before any of his brothers. She read the newspaper out loud after supper, she painted, she wrote poetry, collected butterflies, raised trout in the stock tank. There were those who didn't want Bernice to ever tell story because she'd ooze over that, too. She'd run long and the story overinvolved so we'd end up hearing more than we wanted to hear, if Bernice told a stone.

And then it finally happened, holding a piece of charcoal, she began to ooze on a stone.

"Brother Wodeslaw Gorzechowska was kneeling, he was very troubled in the rude light of this December morning, besides being cold. From his cell he heard the first of the vesper bells. He did not want to go. His head ached. Was it a year now ? Or five ? He did not know.

"Twice he'd asked the Abbot for charcoal and a brazier for the copy garret. The Prior had said, '*Your vow should keep you warm. If the ink freezes, then we will talk charcoal. Brother Wodeslaw, I think your chill is unworthiness.*'

"He tried to be contrite. Still, Wodeslaw believed he could write better and more quickly were he warm. The garret was harsh, now with winter the abbey was a curse on living flesh.

"If beauty is warming, Cracow's Dominican Cathedral ought have indeed been warm. Neither snow nor ice might have fallen on the old city, were beauty warm. For Cracow was a very beautiful city, beauty seeped from every street corner and market post. Everywhere there were statues and frescos. Wodeslaw did not want for beauty, just a few lumps of char.

"In the year of 1654 Brother Wodeslaw Gorzechowska served the Dominican Friary in the Bishopic of Cracow. In the fourteen years since his vow he'd served the learned diocese as a copyist; put more bluntly, a duplicating machine. Sequestered in a high dolomite cell attached to a ganglion of the worshipful cathedral of all the Dominicans, his east window looked over the copper steeples, fortified walls, wet moats and the marketplace of Cracow. In his room Wodeslaw copied in tedious fashion every pamphlet, book and treatise brought to him. Word by word, translating from the vulgate to the Latin, the German, Bohemian and Polish texts. It was dull work, these words of heretics, the unfaithful and the impudent. Some he read, most he just copied.

"If asked, Brother Wodeslaw might have admitted satisfaction for his life offered but one other destination. His choice was either the Church, or to be as his father and his father's father before, a shepherd in the cool narrow valleys south of the city. His father was none other than a good man, but what is a shepherd? What could a shepherd know? Smelling of lanolin and pasture herb, unable to read, what could a man like his father, or his dear shriveled grandmother possibly know? While he, Wodeslaw, gloried among the achievements of the human race, here in the cosmopolitan capital of Cracow.

"*'Our family has always been shepherds'*; his father took an irrational pleasure in that expression. *'Since Julius Caesar we have been shepherds.'* How he had raged when Wodeslaw told him of his decision to take vows with the Dominicans. *'Why a monk when you could be a priest? As a priest you at least live in the community of men, not cloistered in the rock wall scribbling away your life.'* He did not try to explain to his father how the Dominicans were the real power in the church, they wrote the law and for two hundred years had the authority of the Inquisition.

"If only the Abbot could see him a little char for the burner, how much better be his penmanship. Never mind his habit was too thin, designed more for Spain, fair enough in Rome, Bologna and Venice, but not Poland and Poland's winter. How can they expect us to serve the Church with stiff hands? *'Cold is crucifixion. Jesus had an easy death in Jordan. We die daily by inches.'* The heat of his blasphemy warmed Brother Wodeslaw.

"Words were his life. Some were fine words, some fiendish. Ideas and images tumbled from them. And demons. As a copyist the task is not to read but copy. But how to copy and not read? Some words simply refused to copy without holding them first. Dangerous words. Words that tore at him like carrion birds. Tugged at his guts, gouged at his eyes, his mind. To be a Dominican friar was so very dangerous, for if words can trouble the blessed, what might they do to the unsaved? Surely bring madness and sin. Complication is sin. The Bible is enough, that which from the beginning was the word and the word was God.

"Wodeslaw was a copyist and translator from the country tongues. To merely translate is not enough, words need balance. He must know rhythms and edges of meaning. Simplicity is elegance, elegance is grace; a book without grace should be banished, for their writers are confused, fools, sinners.

"The last bell of the vesper rang. Wodeslaw roused himself, went to the water basin, broke the pane of ice and slapped himself with the cold water. Donning his habit he felt warmed, it revived him and he opened the stout oak door of his cell and descended into the stone depths of the cathedral.

"For two hundred years the Dominican Order had been copyists. Providing an important function of transcribing the various languages of the church to the Latin of the Holy See, the copyist existed both as a translater and diplomat, smoothing phrases of otherwise learned men in such a way as to not insult the Holy Fathers or engage their censure. In the advanced year of 1654 it was that almost every word written and published north of the Pyrenees was filtered through the patent offices of the Dominican Order and its huddled clerics.

"Wodeslaw Gorzechowska had made copy, and adjustment, to John Milton's "Defenso Secunda" and "Areopagitica." To Wodeslaw that man was a pail of smoke. There was Friar Nostradomes who, like all Franciscans, was a lot less pail and a lot more smoke. And the mathematical tables of Rhaeticus, something about trigonometry. The Abbot had warned him not to read materials he was to copy. *'Ponder less and copy more.'*

Those were the Abbot's exact words. The man had no pity.

"Among the worst of all to copy was the Pole, Mikola Kopernik, in the Latin, Copernicus, Nicolaus. Born right here in the city of Cracow, 1473. A cleric of vows same as Wodeslaw himself. Secretary to the Bishopic, Copernicus was a pain in the head. He and that fellow Kepler and what's-his-name, Galileo; how they made Wodeslaw's head ache. No matter how he tried to just copy he could not. He knew very well what they were saying. Any fool could see, if not necessarily the Holy See. Copernicus said the earth was not the center, rather only appeared to be. The problem wasn't what Copernicus said. He was after all genteel about it, waiting as he did thirty-six years after writing the manuscript before allowing it to be printed. He well knew the trouble he was making, indeed died before causing it. Which Wodeslaw thought a neat trick considering the consequences on his soul. Galileo was another matter, the old fool was impulsive. No one doubted his observations, had not even unmetriculated students said as much for fifty years? Galileo's problem was he had to put it in print and the Dominicans with their responsibility to the faith had to take action against the old man. Why are writers so impatient? Why can't they relax? It will work out. Give the Scriptures a chance to rearrange themselves, otherwise believers can not help but think Copernicus is right and Joshua is wrong. Given time a method can be found, but not if you are determined to nail the damnable list to the cathedral door with the first light of morning.

"Then there was heretic Kepler, the Protestant. Kepler be cooked if they caught him. It is hard to tell whether he's an alchemist or astrologer, with his five perfect solids . . . why couldn't they be patient? A hundred years is not long to wait, let the Church have time to consider. Therein is knowledge, the rest is speculation and from it faith must be protected.

"After vespers Wodeslaw returned to his garret, one last day of copying before leaving for the country. It had been four years since he'd returned home. While his love of Cracow and the Church was sufficient, he needed now to get away; to the mountains, home and the Veelya. Cracow surely was the most beautiful boisterous city in all Poland. A proud city with its markets and cloth hall, its wealth flowing as the Vestula flowed. Each merchant vessel stopped to offer its silks, Spanish leathers, English oak, Italian books and medicinal grasses; was this wealth that put the stones beneath the churches of Poland's great city. The grey bulk of Wawel Castle and its hen's-foot tower. Wealth and mercantalism rooted the brown stump of Sandomierz tower. The secret as always, thought Wodeslaw, is patience. In this city the very tombs glorified God, its murals, frescos, gold leaf and carved marble. Who could not be a believer in Cracow? This was Augustine's City of God. The gilt altar of St. Mary's, the gothic reach of St. Barbara's, the brooding square shed of St. Mark's and his own great house with its single faceted roof, the broad chancel of the Dominican rising in one leap at heaven.

"'And Copernicus said the Earth moved! Cabbage leaves!

"'Any motion observed in the firmament is not derived from the firmament itself, but from the motion

of the Earth.

"*'Damnable thought.'*

"It did however sound better in Latin. *'Omnis enim quae videtur secundum locum mutatia, au est porpter cocum mutatio, aut est prope spect atae rei motum, sut videntis, aut, certe disparem utrinsque mutatimem. Nam inter mota aequaliter ad eadem non percipitur motus, inter rem visam dico, et videntem.'*

"Latin gave even poor ideas majesty. You could almost feel the earth move; given time these words might even find Grace. Holy Mother, how his head ached.

"The only word in the last letter he received from his mother was, 'Gody.' Wodeslaw knew the meaning. It was both a primitive and insistant invitation to come to Christmas, a Polish Christmas where cares are forgotten and even the chores of barn stall are happy. When family celebrated not only the birth of God but itself. The more primitive believed Gody was the source of the nation and the bastion of the Church.

"Wodeslaw's heart yearned for the uplands, the countryside of his youth. There he could forget Copernicus and Galileo and Kepler and Giordano Bruno and the five perfect solids and what went around what. According to his family, everything revolved around Gody. He could not help laughing to himself. The Church fathers did not understand Gody. How easily they were threatened; the Church will not fall beneath Kepler or Veelya; of course it will be eroded. Do not the statues of the saints dissolve in the rain? So who can live with out rain?

"Four years now since he'd been home. This year

snow had come early so the roads were passable, not the frozen slush and mud of previous Decembers. In a fit of extravagence, Wodeslaw hired a sleigh and horse, and he had presents; thread and needles, a new tang knife for his father, real India pepper, a sash of silk, silver rings for his sisters, a vessel of the finest Algerian lamp oil to scent the house when winter is long, a hand-painted Russian icon on a shingle, and for his beloved older brother who he thought so like himself, a lettered copy of Marco de Domino's "Explanation of the Rainbow," the Abbot's permission was not sought. Never had it been said a personal copy was forbidden. Wodeslaw lettered it the old way with the illuminated characters he'd learned from the old monk and copyist, Brother Kasmir. Bound in Morrocan leather and inscribed, the startling aspect of the chapter was a ready comparison to the Bible. If situated in the place of some obscure chapter, de Domino's Explanation truly fit. That's what worried Wodeslaw. The words of Corpernicus had about them the majesty and mystery of the Mass. In Latin the congregation would have known no difference . . . ahh, but his head . . .

"House Gorzechowska was set back from the mountain lane. The slope below the path was neatly fenced, beyond stood the sheep barn in the shadow of firs, with the steep snow-roof of the mountains. To the uninitiated the barn looked quite like the shingle churches of the region. In the lee corner stood a crucifix, another was fixed beneath the ridgerow. This habit of adoration was common to herders of the region for whom there was no demarkation between faith and practice. The timber house beyond the barn was surrounded by firs and larches.

It rose three stories above the level, the roof blistered by two dormer windows. The roof enclosed an open second floor balcony running the entire length of the house. The first floor was given over to a stone-floored kitchen, attached pantry and central cistern. The opposite end the living space was dominated by an efficient tile stove. A plank bench followed the outside wall where members of the household each had a customary spot, where whittling knife, darning needles, paint-box and dolls remained undisturbed. On festive occasions the clutter was swept away and a gigantic if crude table established in the center of the room.

"The joy of Polish Christmas, Wodeslaw knew, is best practiced on the ecstatic heart. The years of separation coupled now with anticipation prompted his personal rapture. Veelya is a season of the heart, a season for farmers and shepherds, if he was not so sure of friars.

"Wodeslaw thought this as the scents of Gwiaadka, Christmas, flooded over him when he entered the door of his childhood home. The mind does remember smells more readily, more acutely than words. The smell of the fir tree, the hot stove, the bread yeast, the rich leather and fodder smell of his father, the hanging herbs. Good to be family again, to be warm again. Part of some enduring, yet simple thing, this is, Gody.

"The welcome stirred him, Wodeslaw asked if they yet hung the Christmas tree, the *choinka,* in the old fashion, nailed to a hole in the ceiling beam and hung upside down. Neither he nor any knew why, when the rest of Christendom stands this forest tree upright, why do the mountain shepherds of Poland hang the bough upside down? Years before his father said it was so the branches might stay fresh longer. With both the tree and its candies hoisted above reach, it cruelly tantilized the children. Tomorrow they'd argue, which tree is the better, as they search the forest. When they'd finally decide, his father would climb the tree and cut the top. Carefully trimming back all but one branch in the lower whorl so the tree can live to another Christmas. Tomorrow Wodeslaw would shed his monk's habit for the traditional shepherd's clothes, the alpen hat, linen blouse, the leather pants and suspenders, long woolen socks and the durable boots of the hill. The Abbot need not approve, for this is Gody.

"Winter solstice in Poland is ancient, in the upland it is called Czuwac, the rest of Poland knows it as Wigilia, the watch. Of pagan origins, the day is served in fasting. Green boughs are hung about the house. Bread crumbs are scattered on the floor and in corners for the benefit of the household spirits. This is the night that cattle and forest animals speak in human voice to those of clear soul. Meat is not eaten for on this day animals have souls. Before the acceptance of the Roman calendar, the new year began at Wigilia. With the coming of the Church, Jesus is credited with being born exactly on Wigilia night. It is all a matter of patience.

"The men spent the day at their routine tasks, reading omens into every incident, the year to follow predicted, they believed, by Wigilia. Women were busy preparing the feast supper; the babka, yeast cake, pickled herring, the bazzca, beet soup with mushroom dumplings, mounds of small round turnips, pickled carp and trout. The house swelled with the smells of little cakes, blinczyki and perozki, sweet dumplings and the practiced art of oplatek, the wafer bread which with darkness and the first star begins feast night. Oplatek, the breaking bread, is shared between father and mother, brothers and sisters, cousin and cousin, breaking and sharing, each of the other. After the supper the men retired to schnapps and whittling, the uneaten oplatek was gathered up and placed in the mangers of cattle, the crumbs spread around the buildings and along fencelines.

"Wodeslaw knew the Church could not approve of oplatek. Yet had not the Franciscans taken oplatek and created a communion wafer which they sold to royalty at a tidy profit? Holiness is inexact, and patient, he thought.

"After the feast they decorated the tree. Ornaments of painted egg shells, pine carvings, ears of painted wheat, stars of straw, tassels of yarn and silk, dyed weeds, pressed flowers, small sheaves of barley and rye. Over the table was hung "old man dziad" a broad spinning chandelier fashioned from the long stems of wheat straw.

"Slowly turning in the warm air of the house old man dziad appeared to be a swarm of stars. Wodeslaw remembered Copernicus, *'motion perceived is not motion in fact.'* His grandmother opened her kittle box and handed out ornaments she had patiently tied since Martinmass, these the pajak all Poland knew as the grandmother mobiles. Small pyramids, cubes, dodecahedrons, constructed of short straws tied together with string. Some were single geometric shapes, others were of pyramids within cubes within octahedron within dodecahedron, the straw ornaments' complexity a demonstration of her patience and dexterity. Seeing them Wodeslaw felt the physical presence of Kepler, the heretic, and his five perfect solids. When the children hung grandmother's ornaments from the ceiling, Wodeslaw saw not ornaments but Mercury, Venus, Earth, Mars, Jupiter and Saturn. He saw a solar system gathered to the embrace of the sun. Just like that noisy Galileo, the foolish old man who tempted the Inquisition to denounce and burn him, who had seen the same.

"When the swait were hung from the tree and rafter, Wodeslaw was ever so very far away. Swait is scissored from warm, flattened dough, scored and folded until a three-dimensional object results. Cooled, the swait becomes delicate and seemingly impossible to create. Wodeslaw watched as the swaits were hung. Some broke in the hands of children who ate them greedily for good luck. As the swait turned, he watched how the candle light caught them, showing the crescents and phases of the moon. What did Galilieo say, *'the horns of Venus?'* For this the Dominicans imprisoned him.

"Wodeslaw felt as if he had been overcome with a fever and an insistent need to be alone. He begged their pardon, went outdoors and began to run. He did not stop until breathlessness compelled him; staggering he sat down heavily in the dark.

"'Oh, Father, how did they know? How did Kopernik, Kepler, and Galileo know the heavens? Father do I sin when I too see it? Dear God, take this stone off my soul. I do love thee, I do worship thee, but art thou Nature?'

"Below him Wodeslaw watched as the family spilled from the house on their way to the small forest church two miles away. All of them together walking to Pasterka, the dark mass of shepherds. He could not go, he did not wish the parish priest to see him in shepherd's clothes.

"Brother Wodeslaw returned to Cracow after Epiphany. Ten more years he labored over the copy desk. Each Christmas returning whether in mud or snow to his home for Gody. Sixteen years later he, Wodeslaw, became the Abbot of the Dominicans of Cracow. In his administration the monastary acquired the first of many printing presses. In the next two hundred years the Dominican Press of Cracow published thousands of astronomical books, medical texts, civil pamphlets and dictionaries of American Indian languages. At one time half a dozen of its titles were on the Index of Forbidden Books passed by the See of Rome.

"Each time Wodeslaw journeyed to Rome the Holy Father would ask him the elemental questions. *'Dost thou believe in the Virgin?'*

"And Wodeslaw replied, *'Yes, Father.'*

"*'Dost thou believe in the Holy Catholic Church?'*

"While saying his *'Yes,'* Wodeslaw always wondered if they knew how holy and catholic it all was."

The lump of charcoal Bernice held had rubbed off. In the center of her hand was a darkness that we for some unaccountable reason were drawn to touch, and were imprinted by it. We had been oozed.

A Christmas of Faith

aternal acres
summer

King Chickenlegs

Uninteresting. Maybe even dull, was the stone of George. Then it was Uncle Henry's turn again, who had previously told the story of Three Ravens, about a heart cut out. My sister puked. Ed followed and then it was Uncle Jim's turn once more.

"This the very stone," said Great Uncle Jim who, if you remember, was some older than dirt. "This is the very stone on where were crowned the kings and queens of that distant home," he said *hame*. "A stone measuring 27 by 17 by 11 and weighing 450 pounds exact.

"Not quite 450 pounds any more, for want of this small piece." At which Great Uncle Jim undone his transluscent hand and revealed a piece of rock two inches square by one inch thick.

"This is the missing piece, the very one, from the stone Edward Longshanks stole from Scotland in 1295, same who took William Wallace's head off with a meat cleaver. Stole the stone." He said *stane*. "Stole the stane, boldly he did, took it from a kirkhouse yet, and absconded with it to an English smelling place. Was none other than the Stone of Scone he stole from the mossy abbey in Perthshire, in whose absence he installed the right arm and shoulder of William Wallace after having him slew and quartered. Big old stinking front quarter of the man hung on a hook in the vestibule. This to inform the locals that they ought not get involved with intrigue and rebellion. His meat quartered and sent 500 miles apart so as to never get back together, which is a hazard for heaven and why Edward Longshanks did it in the first place. To deprive Billy Wallace of his corporal resurrection, forfeit, because his body parts were spread out so far apart even the drift of a billion years won't put them back together. Not taking any chances, Edward Chickenlegs not only chopped the front quarter loose and sent them parcel post to Scotland, but the hams he sent to the outer Hebrides, the guts of William Wallace he sent to Ireland, the head to East Anglia, the man's thigh he had buried in a crevice in the Welsh Marshes, his gonads dropped in a sea trench off Dover."

My mama hated it when our great uncles took it on themselves to teach us anatomy in close detail.

"Eyeballs and ears to Skye, belly button to Isle of Man, and the right hand of this man Wallace he had boiled in oil and put in a jar in case a miracle befall the parts and the corpse became recomposed by an act of God Himself, he, Longshanks would yet have the most dangerous part of the man, his grievous right hand. A hand that when combined with a claymore was darn lethal to the English. For this, Wallace had proved in stinking piles of good English humanity, piles whose very height might have convinced other monarchs to leave Scotland well alone. Not Longshanks, despite Scotland cost the realm more than it was worth. If Scotland were allowed to float off in a world of democratic intrigue, who knows what violences to the realm might lurk within those borders, consistant with the guiles of the French. And though the Norse had been quiet a century, maybe it was two, they too might find boldness and come night-raiding and burning villages and violating females as was often practiced on the Scots. But what if Scotland proved insufficient? What if they contrived with the Northmen who could swing a battle axe with such keening as to scare the bejesus out of a corpse? What if the French, who knew cutlery, supplied the utensils? What if the morally depraved Irish were enlisted? England would surely die, and this why Edward Longshanks sent the multiple parts of William Wallace's body to forty and eleven different places, including the sea, where even Wallace's great soul could not survive."

"And this why, King Edward stole the Stone of Scone.

"Now you must understand the Stone of Scone was also called the Stone of Destiny; with their knees on the stone, all the kings of Scotland had been crowned there and handed sfter the plough of the land. It was really a sword but plough is what the Scots called it. Any who was not coronated on his knees, on the Stone of Scone, was not a real king. Any rogue could therefore relieve him of his obligation and most likely his head. This of course caused a lot of political stone chasing as a goodly number took kingship on an equally nice stone and thought they were king of all Scotland, the same thought as had occured to some other bloke who kissed his knees to another stone. A modest wartime economy was maintained by this stone-kneeling penchant of the Scots. It kept the armories busy, leisure was reduced to a minimum, it prevented people from complaining about their plight, and it rendered casket carpentry a satisfactory career and few other things. All which came to a halt in due course when people understood the Stone of Scone was special because it wasn't a native stone of Scotland but came from the Holy Land sometime after the Norman Conquest. From Jerusalem lands it came, the very stone which Jacob the prophet had used for a pillow. Why the man had used a rock for a pillow and not a dog is anybody's guess, but there it is. Sometimes the Stone of Scone was called by local folk the Bone of Scone not only because it has a white appearance, like a pillow, but suffers a core that resembles the marrow of bone.

"Edward Chickenlegs took the Bone of Scotland from Scone Abbey in 1295, maybe it was 1299 but somewheres of that time. He had it transported to Westminster Abbey, installed on a parapet surmounted by a wooden throne. There it mocked the Scots for 651 years. The English had their stone, the very one Jacob slept none too well on, that every Scots king was crowned on with his bare knees pressing into this stone, signifying as it did their bond. A white-hued hard stone, it was.

Uncle Jim paused, picked up a toothpick and worked a bit of supper from his tooth. After a moment he resumed the tale.

"Six hundred and fifty-one years since, which is 1950, brings me to Edith Hamilton who was a grandmother, whose daughter was Claire who married James who came to America in 1822 and eventually Wisconsin and started a hotel hard by the Post Road in 1855. Edith had a son David, who also had a son, Ian. Ian Hamilton who was sent to college at Edinburgh and on the night of Christmas Eve 1950 waited outside Westminster Abbey until the night watchman had retired for a nip of cheer from his kit as darkness fell over the Abbey and the likelihood of any disturbance faded. For who but a maniac would be abroad on Christmas Eve when he could at any pub in the country, find a measure of cheer and it most likely free. The night watchman at Westminster did not understand the zeal of Scot nationalism that runs in the heart of the young and the reckless. A zeal to return the Stone of Scone to its rightful place, to carry it off from under the English noses the same as they had carried it away 651 years before.

"The conspirators were three, three of them to remove a 450 pound stone, carry it out of Westminster undetected, across the street also undetected, the stone among them like a stiff dead body. Happily it was Christmas. The police were comfortable, the watchman, too and all of England was likewise. And thus they were able to pick up this terrible anchor, get it out the door, and into the back seat of the car unnoticed. A wee Morris car as did tilt to one side but even this looked natural enough on Christmas Eve, and constables were wont to neglect the scene.

"The theft of the Stone of Destiny was however discovered before the night was out. Police, certain of the intent of the abductors, sealed the border to Scotland, which meant to get its stone back even by an over land carry of the stone, all 450 pounds, of the Stone of Scone.

"Someone blabbed and Ian Hamilton was asked in for questioning. Certain remarks he had made too loudly were brought to light and the police were quite certain they had their man. The night watchman testified this was the same Ian Hamilton who had been discovered asleep in a dim corner of the Westminster, feinting he had dozed off. Which sounded credible enough for who would otherwise fall asleep in Westminster? A conspirator against the realm and the rock? Not likely.

"Hamilton in due course revealed the location of the stone and for his cooperation and recovery of the stone was only reprimanded and not beheaded. Never mind this was now out of favor anyway.

"Which ought end this story except the Stone of Scone had been chipped during the theft, but the area where the chip was broken off was covered over with a solution of cobwebs, old newsprint and oily fingerprints so its absence went unnoticed. None thought to check the returned stone against photographs which might or might not have revealed anything because the chip was from the bottom and the light in Westminster isn't the best. Besides, who but a tourist takes a piture of a stone?

"One of the conspirators emigrated to Canada who lost a bet to a close friend who was of Polish extraction and not having the money to pay off the bet, offered the stone instead. The details of which the Polish friend knew nothing but to humor his friend, took the stone instead of hard cash. The friend had relation in Plover, Wisconsin, who sold farm produce, to whom I sold potatoes. So it was for a hundred bags of white cobbles in 1953 that I received this stone, via Okray Produce, via Canada, via Westminster via Edward Longshanks and William Wallace.

"You know Robert de Bruce took the throne of Scotland kneeling on a stone that wasn't the real thing?" said Uncle Jim.

"How would you like to do what every king north of the borders has dearly desired since 1299? Kneel on the Stone of Scone . . . and this is the very one." With that Uncle Jim quit.

We could not help but stare at the piece of the kingdom held in his hand.

Tamus O'Toole's Tatie Tree

Irish. Loin-cloth, is what my mama called Jacob 'cause as a farmer he didn't amount to nothing, the result of marrying Irish. The Irish was flamed-haired Maureen, freckled as a trout. To her credit she could raise a garden off the steel deck of a sunken battleship. A good garden, if'n mostly potatoes. Was the Irish of her, to raise good potatoes, whether or not the ground cooperated.

Jacob and Maureen lived in a chicken shed, them and nine kids endured if never quite thrived, companioned and sustained by potatoes, three times a day, potatoes. Morning, noon and night, baked, boiled, mashed, poached, roasted. In that house they were called lumpers, fried, salted, pickled, scalloped, gravied, buttered, raw, stewed, floured, toasted, braised. Balloon-sized vegetation were those lumpers, potatoes the size of watermelons, white as an elephant's tusk, one potato fed the lot of them, with left-overs fried in lard for morning's breakfast. Mama said those kids hardly knew meat, it was only potatoes, a few neeps maybe in a real good year, carrots if they were lucky, asparagus stolen from the road side in the spring, cattail roots from the creek, also stolen, and milkweed if eaten young. My mama said they ate robin's eggs at Uncle Jacob's house, that how Irish they were.

The kids grew up, moved away, quickly it seems, they never looked back. Jacob died of horse kick. Maureen did the laundry at the hotel. We saw her at Christmas and baptisms. A small woman with ample hips and her own teeth. She laughed, my mama said, in a sinful way. Meaning Maureen was the Irish, even worse, she was Catholic Irish. My mama thought unwell of the Irish.

My mama didn't want Maureen to tell a stone owing she'd say something papist as might infect the unprotected Protestant child. I think it was because at seventy-two years old Maureen still had a measure of bedpost merry in her. That what my dad said of Maureen. How she rattled poor Jacob's bones and that what killed him, not the horse kick. Mama didn't like my dad talking like that, if we'd said anything so smutty as "bedpost merry" we'd get laundry bar jammed in our mouth, well down and into our mouth, a bar of brown laundry soap so wide, once it was installed, it spread your lips so you couldn't spit it out, all for saying, "bedpost merry."

On the Christmas Eve that Maureen took the story chair, we had oyster stew for supper as is usual for my kind, oysters every Christmas Eve. Maureen brought her chocolate trout, a dessert made of bitter chocolate, flour, walnuts and mashed potatoes, served with sweet whipped cream. Made chocolate chip cookies seem like hardtack in comparison; wouldn'tcha know, my mama had made . . . chocolate chip cookies.

She spoke in a musical way, her voice gentling, like a sleigh gliding over new fallen snow, the words all connected together. As said, song-like and she hushed over consonants like they were vowels and went on like that without ever seeming to stop to punctuate like they was gonna take away the chair if she paused for breath so she commenced right off like a head of water undammed and didn't stop till she was through and the whole of it Irish, which she were. "The damn Irish" according to my mama who hardly ever swore 'ceptin' where Methodists got to. Did I mention my mama didn't want us to hear Auntie Maureen tell her story 'cause she might rub off some of that Irish? My mama didn't trust red-haired women, and them with freckles is the worst kind 'cause it meant their ancestors were heathens a lot longer than they shoulda been and probably cannibals besides.

But Maureen is on the chair already with her motor running, her mouth is jammed in high gear as is distinctive to the Irish. " . . . and you all very well know that Ireland is reknown for storied ministers who put the seven deadly sins to good use. In Ireland story-telling is not prosecutable as a lie. Lust and greed are well-known to improve an otherwise ordinary plot. Lying while at story is no more a sin than God giving baby Jesus to Mary was adultery. For a story, as is good and entertaining enough to hold the darkness at bay and to wind its listeners deep into their quilts . . . is a very very good story, and if lying is what allows that, then it is a worthwhile sin.

"Ireland has great storytellers. James Joyce might

have been the same were he not so over-bite and long-winded. The great story-tellers of 'Eire descend from the period known as P.M., Pre-Marconi: before radio, before the tellie, before ESPN; the deed of it done in the presence of peat fire and a frontier distillate. When a man settled his bairns with another episode of St. Murray and the dragon of East Connick whose serpent was a most voluptuous beast possessing a glittering enamel coat of such a color and intensity that the peep came from leagues beyond just to see the dragon lounge in the sun glowing like a fierce emerald. Granted, a gem stone the size of Kilkarney Castle, not including the tail, and how it was nobody wanted to rid the countryside of the dragon even though there was a standing edict to do so. Said edict to be exercised by every man and boy having a pocket knife . . . notwithstanding, the dragon ate 'em. The upstanding citizens, armed with hedge scissors and toenail clippers, all set off to do their civic duty. On the matter of the edict, the she-dragon of Kilkarney could be no happier, well-fed was she on the lean protein that are Irish folk . . . a most happy dragon be the she of Kilkarney Dells. Sometimes she ate little boys as come and teased her by dancing naughty jigs on her ample bosom which not everybody knows that she-dragons have. This the reason the she-dragon of Kilkarney drew better Sunday attendance than the dull prelate of the kirk. Thousands of wee tweetin' peeps staring down at her daven as she lay in her gown, full and liquid as Jean Harlow who done the same in yellow silk.

"Some believed the she-dragon of Kilkarney died of old age. Others say she were offed by the Black and

Tans. Some thought it was the diocese as done her over by using holy water laced with strychnine same as was done to lascivious popes. A few believe she lives yet among the rocks and mosses of Kilkarney Dells as is sufficiently convoluted to hide a dragon unto the 20th century. And being as folks is watching the tellie instead of traipsing the hills, she isn't so oft seen any more, and with the diminished attendance has had to revert to eating trout and lost sheep and wind-borne cardboard. Her stomach, which is not so much a stomach as a middin heap, can digest anything including old tires and window curtains. Same as choir boys. With but an unregulated belch of methane once in awhile, depending whether or not there's an open spark, produces a prodigious flash that surprises the hiker who unknown to himself is standing on that ridge above the dragon's lair. This the traveler who in perfect innocence lit his pipe and was instantly vaporized save for the heavy duty soles of his shoes. The Park Service having then to put signs on the cliffs above the dells warning of falling over; that being the official reason for the several disappearances in the last years when they know better, what with finding the remains of the man's socks vulcanized to the soles of his former shoes which isn't forensic of a person falling off a cliff.

"Irish storytellers tend to pick on dragons because so little is known about their ecology that a fair deal of interesting stuff concerning their habits can be invented on the spot. This also why storytellers enjoy extraterrestrials, fairies, goblins, ancient kingdoms, Atlantis, and women; with so little evidence to counter-indicate any untrue permutations of the script.

"Relanders as a race relish the memory and time of Finn MacCool, when all the Irish were warriors and grew their hair long and flowing and wore kilts the same as Scots only they were leather with brass rivets and didn't blow in the wind 'cause the hide were thick and the rivets many, the whole ensemble weighing some four stone. Once long ago, they say, all the souls of Ireland were poet-warriors and Celts, in the time before they were Christians, and who's to say whether it was a kinder thing. The Fianna, as those warrior-poets called themselves, did allow none to join the list who could not leap a head-high fence, creep through a badger hole, run up a mountain, stalk a deer with a slingshot, build a fire of green wood, sleep under a snow bank, swim the Dune, rescue a damsel in distress, recite a hundred-line ballad blindfolded with their big toe in a vise while drinking the contents of four washtubs and consume an entire roasted boar cooked but halfway through. All this the members of the Fianna did, hence they weren't good for anything useful like weeding the turnips. And thank God for St. Columba who wandered by to put away the myths that fuel wild poets.

"There is, however, a story of Ireland little known even to the Irish. A quite modern story concerning that time in the previous century called, The Great Hunger.

"The principals of the story are Sir Francis Drake who stole the original potato from the Spaniards at St. Augustine; Pizarro, a Spaniard, having stole the same from the Incas, Indian folk who in turn stole from the Chintak, previous Indian folk. The premium accident here being Sir Walter Raliegh, the same who Drake rescued from dreadful New England, who came home to Ireland

and before disembarking, borrowed a bushel of potatoes for his Irish estate, this being October somewheres of 1586. Within three years Sir Walter was selling the certified seed of this Indian potato, a crop reputed to increase thirty-fold on itself in the course of a single year given no more than the chimney ash and the contents of a chamber pot. A vegetation guaranteed by God, who was Irish, to improve the vigor of every Ireman, increase his potency and restore his youth. The peelings, fried, were even a better fare. This miracle to be accomplished by the most ill-tempered cottage queen using the crudest of utensils over a contrary fire, and all of it more wholesome than manna. Such was the potato's resolution of Irish ways that the vegetable became known among these folk as the potentate, the tatie, the almighty ruler.

"None in Ireland knew of the dying Inca's curse on the cruel Spaniard who sacked their mountain village. The substance being wherever he, or his ill-gotten, did venture, a vile curse was affixed on him and his spoils; on the gold, the feather helmets, the stone idols, the tableware, the virgin girls . . . all of them bearing the dying Inca's curse, *'to all as is bright and proud, on all as is bountiful and green, may the phantom undo.'* Green being the color of the Irish soul, the curse fell most heavy on them.

"Soon after the kidnapped virgins all died of small pox, the feather headdresses molded, the stone idols were misplaced, the tableware rusted and the gold sank to the bottom of the sea. The rest of the curse was saved for the potato, now fully fledged and used by every Irishman who by its bounty fed a dozen children, six of whom wouldn't otherwise have lived to their first catechism.

"About 1845 it began, a time when Ireland was one big tatie patch, and the Irish in such vain surplus themselves as prompted Jonathan Swift to write a modest proposal, it not quite so modest as the title presumes. The civilized parts of Europe were alarmed at the "proceedings" on the green isle whose population had doubled in the near period and was on the way to doubling once more. Inspiring one Reverend Maltus to forewarn in caustic terms of the sorry human condition should this abundancy follow a world-wide pattern, for were not belligerants and revolutionaires made of such ammunition? All the war-monger did require was available in the Irish, only to press them into the service of the frigate and dreadnaught, be-helmet them, drape flags over their coffins when they fall and the world would surely shudder. Give them canvas sail and a steel hull, and an empire so equipped would never see the sun set.

"At this juncture arrived the somewhat delayed curse of the Inca, landing exactly on what Ireland had come to rely to feed its vast, poor population. The bit-folk living in dirt-floor cottages, thatched with straw, and a dull fire to leave the interior carcinogenic, their clothes rough spun, two full dozen of them huddled around one soup pot. All were dependent on the garden beheck the wee picturesque cottage, exclusive to potatoes.

"The Irish, to counter the weight of pressing humanity, had abandoned the neep, the cabbage, the carrot, the brussel sprout, and never looked twice at the dahlia. No other vegetable boomed forth from the ground with the hi-fi amplitude of the Indian kind. None knew the venomous curse as followed Pizarro and Drake and

Raleigh, now secreted away in Ireland, waiting till the time was ripe and the little boys fatted. Then from its lair leaping on mildewy wings to devour its victims by the thousands. And this but an appetizer.

"In County Donegal lived a man named Tamus O'Toole who there dwelt with his kindred of seven peeps and scarlet-maned sheila. When the blight hit that first year in Galway and Clave, it spared Donegal for reasons unknown though Tamus O'Toole felt Galway had more fornicators and skipped-Mass men than good Catholics, and figured as did many of his contemporaries the outset of potato blight was God's instruction to get back to their catechism or next time it'd be brimstone.

"The next year proved either the fornicators had moved or God's aim was bad, because Donegal cellars smelled as putrid as had those of Tipperary and Galway the year previous. Tamus' second youngest child died of scurvy and the rest of the children no longer fit their clothes, and the soup pot was filled with weeds and horse hoof. Assuming Tamus was lucky enough to come across the carcass before his neighbor. It was an awful time, the most regular work was at the churchyard digging graves and funerals so close together no one went to them any more. The priest cut his sermon short to get six more like it done before dusk. To make matters worse, they began dying even faster, so fast the parish priest once calculated if he gave each member the full Catholic rite he'd have to run funeral services non-stop against the sound of the crew digging graves from sunup to sundown. Weren't wood, not even blankets, enough for the shrouds. Infants were simply buried by wholesale lot in untempered holes over which the Reverend wearily made the sign of the cross and walked on to the next.

"Tamus had tended his tatie patch the same as he had the year before, but an evil stink rose up from nowhere to claim his crop of lumpers. To suggest Tamus was a man of science would be inaccurate; like his neighbors he was illiterate with the exception of the ability to sign his name and read a passage or two from the Bible; however he was a keen and curious observer. He noted what folk called the blight was in reference to the insincere method of disease transfer. For out of nowhere came the affliction, as if it was cursed by Moses in Egyptland; the vines took ill with nothing demonstrative to predict the affliction. A healthy plant simply went from vigor one day to rotting blackened leaves on the next. As if a coven of witches had gathered in the air above and their foul odor putrified the earth and all growing things. His neighbors called on a priest to hold an inquistion seeking out the ungodly among them as might be the cause of the blight. Night wives who on broomstick and bones were riding the moondark to spoil every garden and field. For it did seem a curse, as if a phantom was unleashed, and they themselves and the sweet children filling the ground as the once bountiful potato had filled their bellies and cellars.

"Not as the Irish peasant had cellars, the typical method of preserving the crop for the winter was to heap them together in a convenient burrow, cover with straw and an old door. This the Irish potato cellar. No other vegetable kept so well, so solid, so tasteful as the potato.

"Few remembered where the vegetable came from, for it already was called the Irish potato. Ever faithful to the old plot, the peasants had stole it from Raleigh's garden, who after all was English and deserved thieving, for did he not take Irish sweat and spend the worth of it in Londontown on fancy clothes and fumigated women? No better system was ever devised by the agricultural college to incorporate the potato to the Irish habit than to plant this herb in every Orangeman's garden. A poacher who could not find a rabbit for the pot was glad to take home a pocketful of this sweet-fleshed curiosity. When roasted among the coals it tasted so much better than the rabbit.

"If this merry contest proved both good sport and satisfying political redress, it was also true that Ireland was expressly made by God for the potato. In their loam and peat, in coarse sand and gravels did this desparate vegetable joyously take. Add but a bushel of old manure and the faithful eye of that tuber sent forth a pale wand that immediately burst to leaf. In a week it became a tidy bush, by June size enough to eat and if the garden sufficient they did, a second crop already planted, even a third in a single year.

"How many Irish generations had the potato thrived? None really knew or remembered the time when this tuber wasn't part of every garden. From the time of Raleigh's return, less than a generation had passed, and the potato was dearly installed to the Irish, same as clover and blarney. The French would think the potato a curiosity for another hundred years; and the ever-distrustful English noted the striking resemblance of the potato leaf to poisonous nightshade and abhored the same for a century and a half.

"Any sober botanist of the period would have decried the Irish passion for the potato and their increasing dependence. For every botanist knew the book of Revelations is really a disease primer, of plants and pathogens, of hunger, blights and catastrophy. In every growing thing is the germ of disaster, whose time of cataclysm will come. As it did to the Irish in 1846. Hundreds of thousands starved, families, whole villages perished, survivors fled, more thousands died on the road. Relief arrived eventually; wheat from Canada, and a million and a half emigrated to the west. They could have emigrated to hell and found it an improvement.

"Tamus O'Toole did emigrate to Canada with his youngest daughter and her husband in 1874. His dearie had died six years previous and he living in the cottage by himself, though never lonely for the old times because they were so awful.

"In the season of Christmas, Tamus O'Toole tells his story to his grandchildren, how in the year 1847, maybe 1848, he discovered the cure for potato blight. In watching his potato crop he noticed before the vines blackended and died, subtle lesions affixed themselves to the leaves. If the weather proved damp and cool, the lesions spread overnight and by the second day the healthy bush had turned to slime.

"Somewhere in his grandfather's stories Tamus O'Toole recalled a tale from the Fianna called, The Tree of Joy. How once there was in the north a fantastic garden in the keep of a mean overlord named Narob Grubbean who was not only mean to his cattle but mean to his child and wives. He also bit his dog, whipped his horse and kicked his outhouse door. The man was one mean pisser and anybody who liked him hadn't been bit yet. To his field crew he was worse than harsh, sharing with them no bounty, no excess, not even the scattered grain or the sour apple. His keepers were instructed to maim every poacher and to this purpose carried a stone-faced club.

"This grieved the Fianna who were old-fashioned and had taken certain liberties envoked by the poverty of their circumstance, and everyone seemed to think it fair. Not mean Narob Grubbean.

"The legend recalls how wicked Narob was delivered from his ill-humor by tainting his orchard with a magic dust. Not that the Fianna did steal the apples for that be a crime, rather dusted them with earth-borne powder that rendered the apples both beautiful and unpalatable. A powder found readily at the spoil heap of every copper and zinc mine in hard-rock country. A gritty substance that when painted on with quicklime turned the apples an iridescent green. If sulfur was used, a golden dusky hue resulted. What Tamus O'Toole noted in the legend is of no particular interest to storytelling, but science might find it curious. It was not how the apples on mean Mister Grubbean's tree seeemed to take up the afternoon illumination and grow incandescent. Nor was it how the coppered apples shone with a penetrating metallic blue. Neither was it the glimmer and twinkling of them among the branches.

"Not even was it the moral of the legend, how the malevolent overlord on seeing what his tenants had done to his apples realized they might have taken every apple. Knowing this, the great black in his cold heart broke and he was instantly a better man. Which is why this legend is just a legend because everybody knows a nasty attitude can not be altered so easily. In real life people get sued by solicitors or charged with trespass or causing a chemical spill, which may or may not change an attitude.

"According to the Fianna, an amazing thing happened to his Lordship's apple crop. When the autumn rains came early and every other orchard lost a barrel to the mold for every barrel as arrived at the cider press, the orchard of Narob Grubbean did not suffer mold or decay. The price of a barrel of hard cider that year was three times normal, and it might have been a truly awful thing had not Lord Grubbean's heart changed. Where before he spent his profits on cards and race horses, he now supported an orphanage, a free dental clinic, and a public fishing ground stocked with fine hard trout.

"Between the lines of the shop-worn legend, Tamus O'Toole perceived the taxonomic properties of certain earths on various fungi, molds and mildew. What Tamus O'Toole of Donegal thought might also preserve potatoes, if dusted with mineral wastes cemented by quicklime. So it happened Tamus in the awful year of 1848, when blight was raging and all Ireland famished and dying, did lift his tatie crop and paint each and every tuber with a concoction of copper sulfate, and winding a string about each tuber hang them from a rowan tree, in fact, 26 rowan trees, each one festooned, ladened, beset, assailed or as we from a distant vantage might percieve . . . decorated . . . those trees with bushels on bushels of green-tinted potatoes."

Then Maureen in full Irish throat continued,

"Sure it was, the blight passed them by. Any botanist will tell you the reason, on account the copper, zinc and associated minerals of the periodic chart as forestall fungal growth, even if the weather is cool, damp and cloudy.

"Such was the aparition taking place that awful winter, that thousands came in the teeming mobs to see the miracle trees of Tamus O'Toole. The potatoes as withstand the drear host of implacable disease. When all else around was rotting, yet the tatie trees of Tamus O'Toole stood sound as a gold guinea.

"Tamus O'Toole saved not only his own kin but a bushel of close relations, a half bushel of neighbors and a peck of perfect strangers. The soup was thin, the peelings never wasted and the eyes of the lumpers carefully dug out and saved in a broken teakettle to plant the next spring.

"In that part of Ireland Tamus became as famous as the poet-warriors of the lost kingdom of Fianna. If perhaps he wasn't as long limbed nor could he hurtle a spear 600 yards from a sitting position, blindfolded, whilst singing three part harmony to the ancient song of Tillierokken . . . still Tamus could catch a scientific insight where a long-haired warrior with good teeth might miss it.

"At Christmas time in certain untouristed parts of Ireland you can still see rowan trees decorated with what first appear to be glass ornaments. The local pubman's answer to the curious is how it is but a heathen rite with roots in the Celt time. Tourists imagine daring nighttime naked dancing around the trees by eco-freaks . . . which isn't the case at all. If they looked close they'd see the ornaments are not glass, not plastic, not even folded paper, but mineralized potatoes hanging by a string from a rowan tree known for its witching properties.

"Remembered every Christmas in the dales of Donegal is how a miracle, and maybe science, saved a man, his house and his neighbors. How even unto the modern age wherever potatoes are grown, whether in Timbucktoo or the Outer Monogahela, from Michigan and Texarcana, to Blackfoot and Antigo, tatie folk yet anoint their crop as did Tamus O'Toole in that tough year. Remembered is the ballad of the Fianna, the ancient and wild poets who could plow six acres by noon, bale hay the whole afternoon, and sing a poem to it by nightfall. And never once underestimate what an honest lie has to say."

At that Maureen was done. It was almost painful the silence was. The room seemed to shrink. The house too, as if she in her telling had kept it inflated.

Auntie Maureen, widow of Jacob who was brother of Jesse, unfolded her hands. In them she held one small, pale potato.

Chunk of Gravel

Smoke. Uncle Jesse smoked. My mama said this was a bad thing and that Uncle Jesse would go to hell for it. Same as murder. My mama did not want for us to listen to Uncle Jesse. Contamination, she said.

Myself, and don't tell my mama, I loved to watch Uncle Jesse, quirt-eyed as a weasel in a hen house, skinny as a hop pole. Skinny from smoking, Mama said. We thought it Aunt Grace's cooking. We had once had Aunt Grace's chicken. My brother who turned out to later be a lawyer and in that capacity defended some of the finest scum this earth has ever seen, yet cannot abide chicken from the one time eating of Aunt Grace.

It was a prairie craft. Handrolls were. It were manly, not that my mama thought so. It was a skill somewhere between needlepoint and forging bullets, my mama would favor bullets. As an act it summed up the passion of smoking . . . somewhere between lazy and good for nothing. Same as picking your nose.

Watching Uncle Jesse fashion a handroll was a display of the profoundest skill a kid could witness that wasn't sex. A lush movement of the fingers formed the swallow in the paper, followed by a drizzle of tobacco, aromatic as a wet dog. A snake lick at the paper's edge by Uncle Jesse's liver-colored tongue, a fold, a tuck, a seam and it was finished, about the size of a lead pencil. It hung from Uncle Jesse's oyster shell lips like a displaced horn. When lit, his face itself was ignited by the corona of the kitchen match. At that instant he resembled the far side of the moon, cratered by a jackknife, and not a very sharp jackknife. As he smoked he became the Buddha staring out dispassionately at the world.

Uncle Jesse lit the kitchen match using his thumbnail. At the time it struck me as closest equivalent to the art required of a gun slinger. Same snappy wrist action. Same deft thumb as might grace a single action revolver. Same threat of pain and suffering, as the hunk of fired phosphorous bedded under the thumbnail and heck more dramatic to the nervous system than a .48 caliber slug tumbling through the lower intestine at 680 feet per second.

We spent Sunday afternoons out behind the outhouse with a box of kitchen matches, trying for the same viperous motion. Ballerinas did not practice their points and swan-death any more diligently than we studied the thumb-kindled ignition of a kitchen match seen on Uncle Jesse.

Only after we had burnt off most of our thumb did we realize Uncle Jesse had a different thumb. Ours were sweet rounded drumlins compared to his ragged crag.

Uncle Jesse's thumb itself resembled the hammer on a Navy Colt. His thumb worried off in a strange direction not common to thumbs. We were perfectly certain Uncle Jesse could have set fire to otherwise incombustable products with his Lucifer thumb, everything from rotten hay to horseshoes.

My mama does not know it but I have watched people smoke. No where else is the person more honestly meditative, maybe even prayerful. Some people when they smoke inhale, then talk, so the smoke vents in little pulses. Others appear to emit smoke from all sorts of pores. Rare examples never do exhale the charge. There was a time I thought smoke lent a person bouyancy. Smoking before swimming was a good idea, kinda like drown-proofing.

Uncle Jesse's handrolls were basically two-cycle cigarettes, two draws depleted it. Not since have I witnessed the equal of Uncle Jesse's lungs, which could inhale the discharge of a field cannon without ill effect. When he drew on the butt the smolder at the end jerked visibly inward, leaving behind a precarious ash. Loaded, he sat there with the smoke and mused over it like an owl fed too large a snake.

Immoveable was Uncle Jesse. More stature than flesh. Not speaking, not hearing, not even blinking, hoping the snake to die.

All the while the smoke percolated through him. Little wisps of it oozed from under his collar, curled around the bottom of his pant leg. Uncle Jesse was a porous man. His face clouded over, it went through phases, it brightened, it dimmed, he visited his ancestores, he walked on water, he kissed Helen of Troy. I don't know where else he went.

My mama didn't think Uncle Jesse should be telling the Christmas stone since he was perverted. Meaning he smoked. 'Cause he'd stop halfway through to roll one. Mama didn't want us seeing that; she didn't ask our opinion.

When Uncle Jesse got sat down, in his hand was a piece of granite. Everybody knows granite because it is what they make roads of if the town chairman is feeling particularly luxuriant, otherwise it's just plain dirt. Rotten granite they call it, sometimes red granite. If you look at it close, it ain't red as much as pink. Pink and freckled is granite and some cheaper than dirt else they won't make roads of it.

I best warn you of Uncle Jesse's voice. When he tells his story it ain't gonna sound pretty 'cause his vocal cords got frostbite back about a hundred years ago when he was a kid. A horse went down when him and his brother were making wood on a cold day. Stepped in a spring hole, that horse did, and broke its leg and Jesse ran like hellfire two miles and it 16 below at high noon. Should'na tried, the horse was gonna die anyway. Frostbit his voice box and has talked like a crow ever since, all to save a horse some misery. Mama said it from smoking cigarettes; we knew better, was to save a horse even though he knew it weren't gonna happen.

And I shall say another thing before Uncle Jesse begins: people who smoke tell a story different from people who don't. I don't know why but this is so.

Then he began, Uncle Jesse did:

"The old legionaire tugged at his hapless mushroom-shaped feet, Great Zeus how he had abused these feet. He hammered his goblet on the plank table for the wine slave to come by again with the earthen pitcher and refill his cup.

"*'Damndest thing I ever saw,'* he said out loud again, not particular to who should hear him.

"*'Strange, strange sight it was and I seen sights enough to fuel Euripides, I have,'* said in a boasting tone again to no one in particular.

"The slave girl noisily clamored up the narrow stairs from the dark of the wine cellar bearing on her shoulder a handled jeroboam nearly as large as herself. A stout girl she was, with no shortage of expertise and poise, she came straight to the centurian's table and without ceremony tipped the massive jug so a narrow red steam filled the cup to the brim, only the surface tension prevented the liquid from overflowing.

"*'You saucy wench,'* roared the legionaire, knowing it would be he who spilled the wine, a long accepted sign of bad luck as the bare-breasted girl danced away, giggling at the joke.

"With effort the legionaire gathered himself upright and sipped the cup edge till the fluid level retreated below the rim and once more sat down.

"*'Were I a wealthy man I'd buy that girl,'* he yelled to the wine seller.

"*'You, old friend, will never be so wealthy, for I'd sell my wife and children 'ere I'd sell her, for she is the reason my client list is long and old men like you come to tend their wine lip. Not for the wine only, but to see it well-served.'* With that he winked broadly at the legionaire and they both laughed with mutual satisfaction.

"*'So, Gaulus, what strange thing you have seen?'* asked the patron from the next timbered bench. *'You who have seen, and bored us to death, galley ships on fire in the Agean. Who turned our stomachs at the sight of war prisoners thrown to beasts and your ever-so-considerate descriptions of the wars you fought in Germany and Spain and Tunisia. You who have seen all that is peculiar and awful. What has our soldier, our Gaulus seen? For what can there possibly be left to tell for our storied old soldier?'*

"Gaulus sensed the taunt. *'The young,'* he muttered to himself, *'were they not citizens I'd grab them by the cuff and slay them in the alley. They who know nothing, they for whom peace has been so cheap. Thirty years ago when I was a new recruit to the Legion I was sent up-country to a frontier town, don't remember its name. Hick town it was, if still a provencial capital. That the year the edict came down from Rome and Caesar Augustus, how every person in the kept countries was to be counted so the Empire might know the land's worth and compute the tax. Seems the accountants were squabbling over the census and the Caesar, to end the dispute, put the universal census into effect. About the worst sort of bureaucratic nightmare you can imagine. Under the edict every person, whether aged, infirm or suckling babe, was to appear before the polltaker so there could be no fraud in the count. Any who did not was forfeit.'*

"The winekeeper chimed in, *'Complain if you want, I love enrollments; for those two weeks I do more business than all the rest of the year. I sell every jug of near wine and have to buy imported, watered-down peninsular to keep the cups charged. I also rent out my warehouse to the hundreds who cannot find a spare bedbug in town, this when the Caesar calls the roll.'*

"*'It is of such an enrollment I wish to relate,'* the legionaire interjected before the wine merchant could get a second breath and detour the narrative. *'How there was in this distant town not an innhouse as was not over-full. Every shed, pole building, every bath house, tavern and dovecote occupied by country people waiting to be counted.*

"*'I was on a night shift to surpress pickpockets. Rufus, you all remember Rufus, him from the far vulgars, all frecked and red-headdie, who looked every bit the untrainable imbecile but is not a bad heathen once you know his ways. Me and Rufus were guarding the street called the Labbyrrin, as twists among the inns and men's clubs; where the wine is cheap and undilute,'* he said, raising his voice.

"*'Anyway we were minding the store, so to speak, when out of nowhere came this noise as sounded like singing and this with the curfew in effect. 'Course we had to investigate. The inns were closed, the wine shops too, and we heard outloud an uproarous singing. Definitely singing and pretty good singing and not your average wineshop drowning.*

"*'Rounding the corner we saw at the far end of the alley such a scene. Was a stable barn there and from it came a light entirely disproportionate to the source, like a hundred lamps lit. On coming closer we saw there were hundreds of lamps lit, each in the hand of a person, who together comprised a mob, all crowded around this decrepit stable.*

"'I shouted out the authority of Caesar and the crowd parted, Rufus and I marched through them, altogether magnificent in our new military kilts, the brass shining and red capes, the helmets issued that very week still unblemished; a pair we were, strutting the glory of Rome.

"'Great Zeus how that mob smelled. Don't those Judeans know the pleasures of the bath? A little lavender from the uncouth dominions like is the Franks and a person smells less like a chicken coop.

"'Before us was the most domestic scene. Seems outlanders had journeyed to the town in the course of being counted, she heavy with child, I mean heavy. And as everybody knows, not a room to be had. Not even the sleazy kind. Every park bench and manhole cover occupied by a tourist there by the edict of Caesar Augustus. Lord Almighty, when will those bureaucrats learn to do things in alphabetical order instead of one teaming, reeking mob?

"'Course the kid didn't know nothing about no edict; no sooner had the unfortunate couple landed in town than her water broke and they hard pressed to find a burrow. Her man, a resourceful nit, asked at the Inn of the Silver Goblet, that's the place with the Nubian dancers; pretty pricey in ordinary times much less at tax time. Asks the innkeeper if any place at all was available as his stituation was urgent. The innkeeper followed the

guy's gesture to this large round woman on whose face was the look of one holding back the aquaduct by will power alone.

"*'Well, there's the barn,'* he says.

"*'Course Joseph, that was the guy's name, knew this 'cause he had cased out the place on the way down the alley to the inn's back door. Nicest barn in Bethlehem belonged to the Inn of the Silver Goblet, whose many dancers . . . well that's another story.*

"*'What we saw in the stable was his wife had delivered a boy child and wrapped him in carpet and lay it in the feed box. The kid's old man standing off to the side glad to have it done. When some shepherds who happened to be in town for a wool growers' meeting having with them samples of blankets made from their herd's wool. Seeing the couple with the kid they thought to give them a nice selection of sample products they'd only have to carry home anyhow. Was them who started singing, country and western tunes the kind filthy shepherds seem to know, singing real loud, by Jove and the curfew on. Which brought out the curious, each of 'em with their lamp to see what the Hades was going on. All of 'em taking up the refrain of the song about a dog, a horse and a used cart. One song led to another, with this mob of tourists, conventioners, country hicks, pickpockets, street people and regular wage-earning folk who were not yet abed.*

"*'Well, I should have by the authority shut 'em up. Jove Almighty, the noise they made. A civil disturbance if ever I saw one. But I didn't.'*

"The impatient wizen legionaire tapped his empty

cup on the table . . . his narrative almost done . . . *'that a long time ago, and another place. I often wonder what became of that kid in the stable. It was the light of them I remember best.'*

"All that was a long time ago, but light has a way of being recalled . . . smartest thing I ever done was taking this posting at Jerusalem a couple years back. Semi-retirement, the commander calls it. I've got a posh job up on the skull hill; every time there's an execution I'm the guy with the spear. If I think they've suffered long enough, I cut them so they bleed and die off quick. I have seen men bleed to death in the provencial wars and if you gotta go, that's the way, same sensation as when you take a whistling teapot off the fire. That's my job now. Some wouldn't like it but I rather do. Ain't hardly nobody I let hang on the tree, dying that slow means death of asphyxiation 'cause they're lifted off their lungs.

"'I'm told there's some guys gonna get theirs tomorrow, couple thieves and a revolutionary idiot. The thieves I'll help out, what man of us is not a thief whose wallet is fatter than his neighbors. The revolutionary I'll let suffer awhile, can't have that, no sir. Were it not for the strong hand of Rome, the savages be killing each other ten times faster than do we to keep themselves from killing each other.

"'Brother wine, these are dangerous times, and I am glad not to be a road soldier anymore. I thank the grace of Lord Zeus for garrison duty in old Jerusalem.

"' Bartender, one more for the path and I will be kind tomorrow. Fill my cup to overflowing, sir, and when the blood is shed on that dark hill, you will know it is

shed for thee.'

"The jug slave wearily slid over to the now tipsy legionaire, and refilled his cup, the wine well-watered."

At that, Uncle Jesse quit. In his hand an ordinary, if some less than ordinary piece of red granite, the same they make roads and tombstones of.

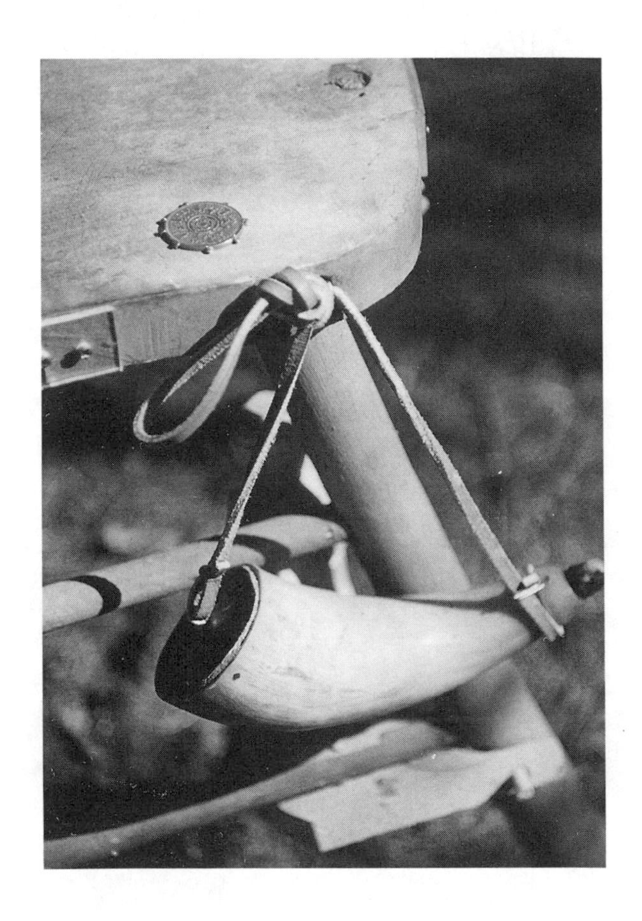

Adah's Last Christmas

Once was not enough for Adah, who told the story of the brick chimney at Charlie's hotel. After all, it was a short story. Never mind that Charlie, great great great grandfather Charlie, was way past dead and shoulda been disremembered like every other mortal person. Adah, his granddaughter, wouldn't let him go off and turn to dust. She remembered him at every possible chance and when Adah took the story chair again we knew we were in for more Charlie.

At the time we didn't understand why Adah hung on to Charlie. It seemed more than pride, as if Charlie captured some vital element that he continued to haunt us, as if great great great grandfather Charlie was central to the endurance of the family. For Adah the world wars didn't matter, the stock market crash didn't either, nor the sinking of the Titantic, not the Lusitania, not D-Day, not the atom bomb, not the Cold War. What mattered in the end was family, the family that must endure, which they will if they remember. A kid had no need of the Lone Ranger or Wild Bill Hickock if they had their own Grandpa Charlie. According to Adah, Charlie was half Paul Bunyan, half Indian chief, a dose of the MacGregors, baked a decent loaf of bread, brewed a chewable beer, and wore a kilt.

In her hand Adah held not a stone but a scrap of cloth, bunchie colored, what some called plaid. We knew enough to call it tartan, meaning it was Scots, same as Charlie.

"The story begins far from here, far from Wisconsin, where that Ojibwa word is no more than another heathen utterance. It begins in London during the exuberant age following the reign of Cromwell, when late in the 17th century a small but foolhardy group of investors incorporated their resources, calling the enterprise 'A Company of Adverturers,' they to risk their fortunes establishing trade with the habitants of Hudson's Bay in far North America. The central figure of this scheme is one Rupert of the Rhine, known more commonly as the Devil's Claw and no less credulously as Prince Rupert. Under his command the Cavaliers met the Roundheads and in due course suffered and murdered for the Crown. With the Restoration, Prince Rupert stood in position of royal favor, his patron rewarding him with a noisome waste annotated as 'that country bounding the bay of Hudson along with all streams leading thereto.'

"It was a deliberate chunk of North America. Notwithstanding its size, no opportunities were to come of it without investment and significant risk, hence the association know as 'The Governor and Company of Adventurers of England Trading into Hudson's Bay.'

"The French were at this same time desirous of similar fortunes. Itinerant traders had long plied the lake regions of New France, obtaining handsome profits as well as compounding their knowledge of the savage interior. None of which was possible without a similar desire on the part of Indian nations who were equally anxious for trade. The French based their enterprise on the experienced traders of Mount Royal, better known as Montreal, their Northwest Company was an amalgamation of French and English, Indians and Scots as well as the intermingled breed that followed these original seeds. The Partners of the Northwest Company were mainly of Scots descent who had been exported to Canada for various criminal tendencies.

"Upstream from Montreal resided a quaint village called Three Rivers, beyond stood only the wilderness and scattered river farms whose steads were carved out of the wilds in a classic pattern. Children born of Three Rivers were quick to acknowledge the river as the central facet of their lives. It was of these, the Montreal men chose the most favored human beings ever to live on the northern continent, those whose lives were legend in their own times. Called *canoemen*, they were the engine in this far-flung enterprise; though it was by another term did they grip history as few other mortals; *les voyageurs*, from the French meaning travelers.

"One ingredient remains, the fur company of John

Jacob Astor and the profoundly American style of wilderness trade. The American Fur Company used an alternative means to secure business; the *courier du bois* acted as independent traders and roamed wherever they wished, although generally outside of the territory utilized by The Northwest Company and clear also of Hudson Bay. The American Fur Company claimed the vast basin from the eastern woodlands and prairies to the western mountains called *les tetons.* In this fashion the American Fur Company obtained with little outlay and overhead the furs of beaver, martin, otter and lynx. Each trader commanding the motive of his profit and success.

"Together these three companies explored and mapped, established communication, transported cargo and built trading posts. They used the civilizations of Indians and with these aboriginal nations formed alliances and by their mutual effort, precipitated a hungry business. The American Fur Company supplied their allies with powder and muskets, and the Northwest and Hudson's Bay did the same, so in time the interior of America became contended ground. It was a conflict not of pitched battle, rather a more insidious thing as variable as gentle banditry and pilferage to kidnapping and murder, all conducted in the surplus obscurity of the wilderness.

"Those who ventured the interior did so without vanity for their lives. Many were the entreprenuers who cast off from the docks of Montreal never to return. Some took measure of the monster forest and fell back broken. Yet slowly it happened, the dim reaches were given names and those who followed had the new security of a baptized place that even timid souls might follow.

"The American Fur Company traveled the western course beneath the Great Lakes while the Northwest and HBC entered the continent farther north. HBC called their trading posts factories and dotted the rim of Hudson's Bay with places like Moose, York and Churchill. The NW Company evolved a system of canoe fleets, one set capable of navigating the big lakes in bark canoes driven by sixteen voyageurs bearing a ton of cargo. At Grand Portage they exchanged trade goods for fur bales from the interior, where smaller river canoes carried the business into *du pays den haute*, the hinterlands.

"The American Company was decidedly the lesser of the three companies. Their trade network had a loose, disjointed aspect, utilizing independent traders, scouts, mountaineers, outcasts and breeds with which to scour the plains and mountains. They penetrated to the lair of the Blackfeet, established the trails to Oregon and California and thus performed civilization's bidding while keeping themselves at arm's length of it.

"Quite by accident an unclaimed hollow formed between these combines, it is of this place my story concerns.

"In 1814 the Treaty of Ghent formally ended the second war between the British Empire and its distaff colony; despite the end of hostilites, treaty negotiations proved difficult. Following the war the British had what seemed to the Americans a ridiculous charity toward the aboriginals, with particular interest shown to an area northwest of the Ohio, a region the British had resolved to maintain as a refuge for displaced Indian peoples. Spokesmen for the colonies were impatient with what seemed a sudden onset of conscience, the American belief was those preferring to cling to heathen proclivities would find succor in the extensive wilderness without the application of an Indian preserve. The representatives of the Crown continued to urge this consideration. Time, they said, will prove more relentless than the will unless provisions are made for Indian peoples, without which the natives will surely disappear from the earth as if they never existed. That, many Americans thought, would not be so bad.

"Wisconsin," Adah went on, "was at the northern extreme of the old Northwest Territory being argued over by the peace commissioners at Ghent, bearing the name given to it by the *courier du bois, ouicosee.*

"About halfway up a river of this same name was a rocky shallow; where stood a post of the American Fur Company. A sumptuous habitation by 1840 standards, while not as expansive as the fort at Grand Portage or the white-washed factories of the Hudson, instead a gathering of crib logs and thatched roof. It was nevertheless a marvel of hospitality, for it was one of the few habitations between Lake Superior and the Winnebago Portage, between Fort Hennipen to the west and Fort Howard on the east. The establishment's chief was a wide dark French Canadian named John Baptiste DuBay.

"The fur empire was by this time in decline, largely because the region was 'trapped out.' However to the less appraising eye, before them was nothing else than an indolent wilderness. Such was not the case, for the place was mined out of fisher, otter and beaver. It was now in this region a hard labor to gain a living as a fur trader.

"If John DuBay knew this, that the woods was empty of prospects, he did not show it. A stout man with shoulders wide as he was short, as dark in complexion as an Indian, with long hair, wearing a loose shirt and baggy leather breeches with moccasins on his feet. DuBay's eyes had the mischievous luster of French Canadians. He enjoyed the trade and pleasured in the daily life and contact with Indians, the strange, almost leisurely methods of the fur trade; the barter, the storytelling, the cud-chewing, the control of frustration when it comes to dealing with the unlettered but cunning native. The son of a woods runner, his father had, as was the habit, married an Indian bride as much for business as for more familiar needs. As a child John Baptiste heard and well-learned the stories of voyageurs, the legends of the bark canoe, the big lakes, the rivers, the blackflies, and the long and suffering winters.

"Great great great grandad Charlie, lived next door to John DuBay. In 1840 the interval between them was sixteen miles, that but a day's walk following the path along the river. Charles had come to Plover precinct from Michilimackinac where his father had been employed as a clerk to the trade. His grandfather Angus Rice had served in the Frazer regiment dispatched to quell the American troubles. The father of Angus was also Angus but the surname was not Rice but MacGregor of the keep and line of MacGregor." Adah said the words in three encrusted syllables, said it so the word "MacGregor" kind of hung in the air like a dry fly is supposed to.

"For three hundred years," she explained, "the MacGregors followed their proclivities in Scotland, hostile proclivities, together commiting more acts of vandalism and theft than any other clan in the isles. They were not very nice people. Rob Roy was a MacGregor, he was not nice either. The British government's response at first had been exasperation, finally extermination. The Lord's Council banished the name MacGregor from public and private list as well as casual utterance. That name could not be written, spoken out loud or put to land deed. Any found using the name were imprisoned, transported or hung. Angus MacGregor took the name Rice for the sake of irony. Rice being the Scots word for the torn off branch used to fashion hedges or kindle a green fire for smoking salmon, it most likely a poached salmon. Green fire, slow and smoky, is the only way to cook trout.

"Charlie Rice and John Baptiste DuBay knew each other in the perfunctory fashion of the wilderness. In 1840 in Wisconsin those who lived within a hundred miles knew each other like the best of friends. It was on a trading venture to Fort Howard that John DuBay stopped at the tavern of Charlie Rice. November is late for such a journey but not overly difficult for a man of DuBay's robust nature. Others might have preferred a horse, he walked believing he could out-distance a horse given the trail conditions, besides keeping all his innards in place, as is unlikely on a horse.

"The weather had turned foul as November is wont, the slow drizzle evolved into a steady freezing rain, then heavy wet snow, enough even to make a voyageur gloomy. A man of careful economy, DuBay planned to spend the nights in the woods beside the comfort of a fire. Such was still his intent when he topped the sandy rise on the river at a place called Yellow Banks. He had there a change of plans.

"In the distance stood the inn-house of Charles Rice on the lee side of a prairie. A brave house of sawn whitewashed lumber nailed over hewn walls, it stood two full stories with real windows and a magnificent brick chimney whose like was not to be seen this side of the Illinois.

"Charles Rice maintained an inn, while it was not the only trail house between Fort Howard and what lay westward, it was the most accomplished. In later years folks came to believe Lincoln had slept there, which wasn't true though Jeff Davis did. Without intent the Rice tavern became tangled in a variety of tellings, most of them untrue, the interesting ones involved local mischievousness such as the time the Winnebago stage was robbed and the felons were thought to have gathered their plot in Rice's tavern and hidden the stage box in the dirt floor of the livery. Or how Maria Sweeney, the famous window smasher, was given accomodation on her fame alone, that she might leave the windows alone. There was the cheated lumber jack who shot one of the Curran brothers in the middle of his imported plate glass mirror, a double homicide it was: killed the man and the mirror. But all these events belong to a future time. What Monsieur DuBay saw was that chimney smoking in a beckoning way, on a forlorn and chill November afternoon; he decided to take supper with Charlie. Fort Howard could wait.

"A stranger coming unannounced through the door of an inn house is no curiosity, but a small man of John DuBay's dark wild proportion is however disconcerting. The door was flung open before him, aided by the wind, as a result slammed against the plaster wall sending a framed picture of George IV to the floor. Charlie taking innocent pleasure at the fire was startled in spite of himself. Seeing the storm-sodden figure at the door, he bade him enter ere the dark day suck the warmth of the house. DuBay complied, hung his traveling cape on a row of pegs and sloshed in his moccasins to the fire.

"'*Shuck your wet hide,*' said Rice, '*you're the very picture of misery.*' With that he bid a child servant bring a woolen blanket with slippers and watched as DuBay before him exited from his over-burden, at length reclining in the deacon's corner with the blanket wound tight about him. A silence passed, Rice directed more wood to the fire. The place was quiet except for the sounds of the kitchen and upstairs chambers, of footsteps on the floor, sounds of a bed being made. John DuBay knew he was fated to spend the night.

"In an incidental way Charlie turned to DuBay and introduced himself, followed by an equal remark from DuBay, with it they were satisfied. DuBay was brought his supper and a hot tonic with some evidence of whiskey. A look out the door disclosed the November inclemency unabated, complete was the change to snow now falling with a vengeance. As the daylight waned Charlie Rice and John Baptiste DuBay talked of their affairs. The reference in their conversation that concerns us is the chance mention of the mutual employment of their fathers with the Northwest Company. The subject broadened, the cups were filled, the fire tended and in a short while these two were clapping each other on the back in a fit of foolish remembrance, regaling each other with stories they heard told of the Company. In particular was their recollection of Christmas as enacted at the posts.

"Nothing in their minds was ever so grand, so festive, so alive as Christmas done in the style of the Partners. The consequence of this recollection being DuBay's invitation to Rice to recreate it, once more would they make Christmas the old way at his post on the Eau Plaine a month hence. On this they shook hands.

"With morning DuBay was gone, in typical woods fashion departing with first light in order to make the most of the short day in that season.

"My story," said Adah, "is just a ragged memory of by-gone days when the fathers of us were young and the customs of this unsettled country were loose. "There is," she went on, "some embarrassment to admit our ancestors were playful men. It was after all a make-believe Christmas these two contrived, something Sunday School children might enact, though it was not made of children and certainly not of Sunday.

"It is nevertheless true. My father said it was so and he never lied. The formal invitation from DuBay was lettered on a card of birch bark.

"'A fortnight Christmas,' it said.

"'DuBay Post,' it said.

"'On the Ouicosee at Eau Plaine,' it said.

"The card was delivered by an Indian courier who remained to help Charlie Rice move his substantial brood the sixteen miles upstream to the DuBay Post. December that year had been cold but clear. Snow was delayed as is sometimes the case in the interior away from the lakes.

Charlie now felt distinctly stupid, how foolish it was to spend time on this . . . this theatre. A grown man with bairns to look after and Mrs. Rice thinking him a little outta kilter to go trapsing to the Eau Plaine for a Christmas party. But the die was cast; if DuBay hadn't sent the rustic invitation, he would have forgotten the whole business. Now he only remembered the toad-eating grin on their faces as they shook hands at the compact a month previous.

"Late on the afternoon of December 23rd, they trudged over another sandy dune. On the next knoll, intervened by yet another swale of cord grass and cattail, stood the outstead and buildings of DuBay Post, situated that one stucture led to the next and in their angles formed a sheltered interior court. The foremost structure was obviously the principle trade building; various traps, boxes, flour bags and Indian items were hung and stacked haphazardly about; snowshoes of the Ojibwa design, hide stretching frames, copper and iron kettles. Inside was the plentitude as comprised the fur trade; buttons, needles, thread, scissors, knives, iron strap, soap, bolt cloth, hymn books, lead, cornmeal, phosphorous matches, mirrors, eastern shoes, hats, blankets, tobacco, gunpowder, baking powder and glorious salt. Taken together these items defined civilization to Indians and homesteader alike.

"The dwelling of the DuBays intersected at right angles with the trading hall, connected with a plank door on iron hinges. The living room had a mortar and stone fireplace topped by a stick and mortar chimney. The subsequent buildings were linked by doorways for convenience and bad weather. A shed that passed as the barn kept chickens and a real milk cow whose resource had saved numerous Indian babies whose natural mothers died or could not nurse. Despite the look of prosperity, the DuBay Post had been eclipsed. With the reduction of the fur trade and the withdrawal of the American Fur Company to the more western beaver grounds, posts like DuBay's were passing out of their glory. The disintigration of Indian peoples added to the decline, amid the pressures of a relentless white settlement just then beginning in Wisconsin. John Baptiste DuBay in his heart knew another decade would end a pattern that had ruled this forest for nearly two hundred years. For a century and a half his family had been woodsmen and voyageurs in the most satisfactory enterprise imaginable; now he was the last. It hurt as few emotions can; a way of life, a good way of being, was ending. Who beyond a few traders and Indians understood what was dying before their very eyes? And for what? More land for the plow? Holy Mary, didn't they understand what they were doing? Already he had seen the cruisers and Maine yankees, listened how they talked in excited tones of wealth to be cut and rafted down river. They had already emptied the forests of Maine. It's a bonanza, they told him, best to get in on the ground floor or the rewards will pass by. Let them pass. God damn let it; by then he'd be cleared out and safe in another decent wild place where they couldn't touch him.

"Behind the barn was a pen for pigs that spilled the wonderful aroma of the sty to every eddy and shade in the pines. To the side of the pig pen stood a garden for turnips, carrots, French cabbages and beans. Beyond was a canoe shed where an old French-Cree from Fort William fashioned bark canoes that the post sold for three dollars each. Spritely, bounding canoes. One fathom and two, birch and cedar and white pine pitch, by the hand of Ignatio LaBreque, cousin of the famous voyageur, born to a white-toothed Cree woman whose husband died of Carrier's disease. Ignatio was bent over as a crimped nail, with sinewed hands taut as muskrat traps, with a little crooked knife and a kindling axe he made canoes. Smoked a clay pipe, sang songs to himself, and made canoes. Elegant, buoyant, breathtaking canoes. Canoes for trappers, cruisers, soldiers, missionaires, canoes for rice gathering.

"A granary stood on poles where they stored cob corn for grinding into meal. By his own estimate DuBay figured he had twelve acres planted to corn; a good thing, the corn. It stored well if you kept a bobcat leashed in a dark hole beneath the poles to catch the mice. People no longer starved during a hard winter as they had before, five bushel kept a family alive if snow came early or it turned hard cold. Fish nets, clam rakes, spawning spears; it was a good and holy life at DuBay Post.

"The house of the trader was not so crude as the rest of the buildings. The interior walls were hewn smooth and both interior and exterior had been whitewashed. The main room was fronted by a mammoth chimney with two flues, one for heating, the other served the backside of the kitchen as an indoor oven. The low timbered ceiling gave the long wide room a claustrophobic sense, more a coal mine than a dwelling. On the wall hung coats, trade blankets, a picture of what looked like a musketeer, snowshoes, traps, a trace of bells, miscellaneous powder horns, jerkins and pouches. At the end of the room was a ladder tilted into a sleeping loft.

"What surprised Charlie Rice was the number of people apparently living near the post, he had counted four family groups in separate camps. The place was not only a trading post but a community whose activity level had all the aspects of a village. Long before they caught sight of the post they had heard the children and smelled the peculiar scent that abides with aboriginal places. Their courier yipped loudly when they broke through the trees and found themselves immediately surrounded by dogs, half-naked children, greasy adults, all manner of boys, maidens, each seemingly intent on going through their pockets, inspecting their hands and touching their hair.

"John DuBay knew an hour previous the whereabouts of the Rice party, the methods were Indian and a matter of good policy for a Company man. As he stood at the porch waiting he didn't feel the same foolishness Rice was so aware of. He had fewer reasons to sense any foolishness; this was Christmas after all, and one of the last. What did it hurt to raise the spirits of voyageurs and partners one more time? Though surely he knew what it hurt, for what memory is raised and enlisted, must then be put away again, and such memories do not retreat so peaceful as they come. Perhaps it would be wiser to have a normal Christmas, a modern Christmas and leave the old wine corked. If John DuBay committed himself to that resolution he forgot it by the time he put his bear-hug around Charlie and physically carried Mrs.Rice the last fifty yards to the door. She looking at Charlie with faint horror and accusation . . . *'Now what hav' ye got us unto Charles!'*

"Christmas Eve day was spent in preparation. Firewood was gathered from the surrounding forest, wild game dressed and reduced to roasting pieces or added to the monumental kettle doing its business in the front yard tended by a venerable-looking squaw whose face appeared to be both tattooed and quilted. The bread ovens spewed aromas of the divine, a young boy hunkered on his heels on the edge of the veranda peeling cattails. Other children were cutting boughs of cedar to hang from the walls and pile in corners for luxuriant couches. Some were wetted and burned to scent the air. Mistress Rice demonstrated for the wild bairns how to weave garlands and wreaths from boughs. They were, all of them, caught up in an old, old dream.

"Night fell. The fires were raised, candles lit as well as the one fabulous oil lamp. As if knowing the occasion perfectly, the Ojibwa and the Menominee and a straggling family of Sioux went to their bundles and unwound their dancing clothes, their fawn skins and mink tails, beaded moccasins, feathers, bells and amulets. The women painted their cheekbones in blue earth, their ears in red, their breasts they powdered with sugar. From their cherished belongings they brought forth their pipes, their medicines, and their story rolls. How well these people knew Christmas, who had better reason, for before them lay a long and uncertain winter. Often they wondered among themselves if any white man except the wild French knew how to sing and catch hold of the tail of December's joyful feast.

"John DuBay dressed that night in a pair of velvet

pantaloons, black boots and a white linen shirt. He was beautiful, for a wild Canuck. His brown wife wore a full length ivory gown, breathtaking against her complexion, she of dark eye and meat-eaters teeth.

"It was for this they conspired, the madrigal of the forest, a chance to roast the pig in the front yard and dress like the Partners of the Old Trade. To do Christmas as did the winterers of the old, as it was in the forts and factories, in the place of Cree and Ojib, and Fox and Dakota and Potowatomi and Menominee, of winterers and carriers, those legions of sinewy men with banjo wires for legs. Tonight Rice was no longer the remnant of a broken and scattered clan, not the child of an indentured clerk. This night Rice became again the MacGregor, this and the ever more ancient names, Griogaraich and Red Mackracher. He wore what was meant to be worn by men who were men; Charles Rice MacGregor tied on his family, tied on the lineage of five hundred years. When his grandfather shipped out on the Clyde he carried with him a bolt of cloth, fourteen yards of a remnant worn by those who equally loved music and war. A cloth of muted color, fourteen yards it was, the making of three kilts in a passage trunk. Of all else where the family had spent the last two thousand years, nothing remained, not even a name.

"Charlie didn't really know how to sew a kilt, but he did fine enough. With long stockings, Indian moccasins and a linen shirt it was a forest version. How natural it felt wearing it, he immediately understood the family's strange old attachment to raiding parties. For the garment had in its very nature a swagger, it felt like a cocked gun, of something not quite sane or sober, certainly not

Presbyterian and never honestly civilized.

"With our participants enrobed, my story nears its end. That Christmas Eve at DuBay Post they danced, they touched cups, they sang old songs, French songs, Indian songs. They danced on the timber floor and danced in the snow. They sang and danced and kissed their wives, their children and their neighbors. They touched cups again and again. They sang a mixture of languages; Quebecquois, English, Ojib, Memomin, Gaelic and Scots. They ate and told more stories. Long stories, quiet stories, laughing and crying tales, all of them true. They passed pipes, appeased, thanked and congratulated the gods and touched their cups once more. They ate and belched and cupped again. Babes and children fell asleep, friends and neighbors, too . . . in boughs, in corners and in blankets. The survivors talked and tended the fire while they continued to touch their cups. Morning finally came and John Baptiste DuBay and Charlie Rice MacGregor were still talking if at a reduced volume and coherence. Then they, too, fell asleep.

"It was on or near the first of January of the new year of 1842 when Charlie Rice and Missus walked the sixteen miles to the sandy bend of the river. It was a thoughtful walk. Charlie knew they had participated in a Christmas done the forest way. Yet surely, he thought, generations hence they will still do such things. Will not the pinery yet be so proud as to forbid the timid? And will there not yet be Indians and wolves, pigeons to roast and a million acres of wild woods yet? Given there will be cast iron stoves and window glass, but what else can change?

"Charlie lived to see the railroad, the last of the

passenger pigeon, the end of wolves, the last fabulous white pine tree, and he saw concrete come. He died on the Moore Hill overlooking the outwash, while picking blackberries. It was August. At the house auction your grandfather bought from the estate a plain pine dresser. In the bottom drawer was ten yards of plaid cloth, I mean tartan," Adah said.

Adah died the following year for her heart was bad. The week previous she had been taken to the hospital. The second night she dressed herself and walked home, sixteen miles. She was after all Charlie's granddaughter. Took to her bed and died in the bedroom she and George shared for fifty-three years. Covering her bed were those ten yards of MacGregor.

They Once Were Boys

Calamity. Uncle Jim lived to the age of 94. He outlived all his brothers and sisters, he outlived horses, and the agriculture made of horses. He believed horses were how God intended agriculture to proceed and any departure from this ordinance would result in not only calamity, but a deserved and holy calamity.

I have explained before, Uncle Jim lived down the road where he farmed a million years, or some similar time. Farmed that whole while like God intended farmers to farm, with horse. Belgians, Percherons, Clydes. Horses the size of mountains, some more mountain ranges than mere mountains, a few snow-capped and volcanic.

Born in 1872 Uncle Jim had no way of knowing that calamity was on the way in the guise of various machines and would in his lifetime render of agriculture what the machine did to other simple crafts. For a person who had sworn true fidelity and honor to the equine, the result was not mere calamity.

However, this is a Christmas story, and more than that, this is a stone story of the kind duly and reverently practiced by my family since the most ancient days. A practice engaged by any participant willing to form their tale around the circumstance of a stone. A stone that was by the story transformed. A stone that started out its career as one of God knows how many quadzillions of other nondescript stones, but by the application of a seasonal mirth was made special. Never mind the underlying moral, that deep down underneath it was still a plain stone. Beneath this moral was yet another, that all as is woefully ordinary is by the application of a story, transformed. Telling a story, whether it was the truth or a rightful extension of the truth, was the entirety of what constituted goodness in the universe. Uncle Jim, about to tell a stone, took the honored seat.

On the story chair every year taken from grandmother's closet and set in the middle of the parlor each participant commenced in honored recitation, always beginning with . . . "this no ordinary stone is . . ."

Uncle Jim told a stone story for the last time in 1964, that year he died quietly in the farmhouse he built a half mile south from his brother George. Died in the upstairs bedroom on the east end of the house, where the window framed the morning light in a pleasing way. Uncle Jim was one of the last of them, the last of their time and experience. His voice shallow as he spoke, spittle forming on his lips.

He spoke slowly as might be expected, the words interspaced by long pauses, for breath, for recollection, perhaps out of some painfulness itself.

The old, we were told, are subject to melancholy, this my mother explained as if to warn us of the mood as might prey on Uncle Jim. She meant for us not to snicker, not to fidget or complain that the story was not like one Captain Kangaroo told. Uncle Jim's story would be halting, inexactly punctuated, it would grow vacant for no reason, it would not connect time logically. "Just listen," she instructed. Actually, it was a warning. "Listen, listen, listen . . . for he is one of the last to speak of a time when he like you was a child. Listen, dear children, for what Uncle Jim speaks will soon go forever still. Sit. Be reverent, and . . . listen!"

"This no ordinary stone is," saith the Great Uncle Jim, in a voice that was less spent by vocal cords than the rattle of gravel in a wheelbarrow. In his hand, the tiniest arrowhead ever seen.

"I was twelve in 1884, a middlin' year on the farm of my father but for the early winter. Snow commenced at Thanksgiving and didn't quit. Not that it mattered, for the traffic to the hotel was at a minimum come winter. Roads disappeared, freight of any volume was impossible, companies moved cargo during the summer and fall, and put up for the winter, the sleigh the only option. The cold effected the teamsters and was equally brutal on the horses. A sleigh once loaded had to keep moving for the weight of the runners melted the snow and ice, which thereafter froze, locking the sleigh in place if it paused for any length. It then to be broken loose in order to move off. Light sleighs and bobs transported people, mail and parcels, but freight by the ton in open country was ended until the following summer. But when it did resume, it was in a swarming volume, many days overwhelming the hotel that we looked forward to winter's return for the simple leisure of it.

"It was my job as a child to tend the horses of those who stayed at the hotel. From the yardway I took them to the barn, saw that they were watered, blanketed and stalled. My father wanted all the customers' horses curried so they came to harness the next morning looking fresh. It was, he said, good business. From an early age I was disposed to horses. Though there were other chores about the hotel -- tending the wood pile, washing the linens, supplying the kitchen -- but I preferred the barn and its chores. The horses were better company than my sisters.

"As said, the winter arrived early, traffic on the road slowed, trickled and then with more snow, ceased completely, days passed when we had no trade. To keep us occupied my father sent me and George to the low woods to make firewood and refill the wood shed. Making wood was never-ending for we burned wood in the kitchen stove, wood in the parlor stove, the taproom, the laundry, the smokehouse, wood in the iron shop and during the depths of winter, in the pump house. Father, to insure our devotion to this occupation, sold stovewood by the cord. Many drove from the village to purchase it, or we delivered the wood to them. Neatly stacked at Mr. Pierce's meat market, who took a cord of new maple every month for his smoke house. He was particular about it, didn't want the over-dry that it might break into flame, as don't do hams and sow belly any favor. No sticks over four inches in diameter and none under two and a half. All stacked crisp as Sunday shirt in his wood rack; 'Mind, sweep the bark afterwards.' Mr. Pierce was a hard customer but regular. For this our father charged one dollar a month of which we got a shilling each. He telling us we were overpaid.

"Did I say firewood was a hateful chore? It was also, as I now remember it, a heavenly and wondrous chore, for George and I were by its release off to ourselves in the woods, off in the wild without a father, mother or sister in sight. Armed with an axe and a harp saw."

Uncle Jim stopped for a moment, the look on his face was lonesome, least we thought it was lonesome.

"When I was a child, the preacher told us on entering heaven we'd all get a harp to celebrate the Lord. I did not know the harp to be the musical instrument as was his intent. The harp I knew was that implement my brother and I took to the woods to cut the endless stovewood. I was as a result uncertain of heaven, if it was but an eternal commitment to a chore I had already well enough exercised. But the more I thought about that heavenly harp, the better I understood what was meant. The harp saw meant that heaven had woods, and if it had woods, surely there were creeks and running streams, with muskrats, otter, bear, fox kits, owl nest, squirrels and a scissors lock .22 rifle and some matches. Hence I came to think well of heaven, a nice place even if it had chores attached. Eventually I learned of my mistranslation; the harp the preacher spoke of wasn't the bow saw but a musical instrument. So heaven lost its woods and streams.

I have accepted if the Lord wants me to sing, I shall; in truth I'd rather cut wood.

"George and I were at every chance off to the woods, the woodpile demanding our constant attention. In those days a woodpile was like money in the bank; you could never be too wealthy when it came to stovewood. Besides, our father bartered it regularly for supplies needed by the hotel. The price of cured firewood rose during the late winter when those in the village and nearby farmers ran short, a sleighful of dry wood meant more to the keep of a family than whether they were eating beefsteak or cornmeal mush. Especially if we got snowed in.

"We were off to the woods several times a week, except during the summer when there was haying and wheat and potatoes also. In the early spring the entire family sailed for the woods. I say sailed because mire was on the land, not solid ground at all, so it was we sailed for the woods. Our mama didn't much care for the woods but sugarin' was different; she allowed herself to venture there at sugarin'. It was not work as much as it was watching, watching the boil, and we ate so very well. George and I learned to cook pretty good for kids; we'd seal a length of stovepipe at each end with a block of wood, fill the pipe with beans and molasses, most of a side of bacon, bury the business in a hole filled with hot ashes, cover it with more ashes, four hours later extract the bean pipe to sup our parents and sisters on the best fare you could ever hope, baked beans pungent as summer tarpaper.

"Other than at sugarin', it was just George and I in the woods. We followed the trace as went south from the hotel, crossed over a creek about a mile and a half along, a quarter beyond we followed another creek to a range of low sand hills and there an old lonesome stand of woods. In that time Indians were still about, they kept camp on the marsh, below the creeks, and were in this way to themselves. They came and went with the summer, a few stayed through the winter but at their peril for the winter was harsh in the ranges. In the marsh and its obscurity, who knows whether they survived, we did find traces of their camps come spring, never knowing whether they lived or died.

"George and I learned what civilization is: documentation. The Indians were unlisted and unbaptized; here were people whose name had never been written down, a doctor never gazed down their throat, no bill or lein or mortgage had their name on it. No land either. Civilization and everything civilization means is summed up by the naming. We give all manner of reverence to things because it has a name. What makes a savage is namelessness. Our births are listed, our baptism, our marriage and our deaths, even if it is heaping death the likes of Shiloh . . . all are listed. For even if we pile ten thousand into a trench and shovel them over, corpses too blown apart to collect, too bloated or fly-infested, still we list them, knowing the great sadness is if a thing lives and dies unknown.

"We often encountered the Indians, hapless little bands who for one reason or another did not return to the wintering grounds at Poygan on Lake Winnebago. Their reasons were variable; an infirmity that precluded travel of one who would in the next week die in the woods, then wrapped in a blanket and buried among the dunes, or if the ground was frozen, nestled in a crude nest in the crotch of a tree. Once the ill member of them had died, the remaining group traveled over land via the marshes to the open water of the Fox and Wolf rivers. Life was easier there at Poygan than trying to survive winter in the interior. Still some remained, for reasons of illness, injury, advanced age, or pregnancy. It is well known that native women could bear a child behind a clump of lilacs and none be the wiser. Still there were some proprieties observed, even by these folk. A newly freshened woman is capable of travel, as is the child, but at some peril.

"This was the reason a group of six had elected to remain in the woods nearby where George and I were at our wood cutting. They had not removed to winter at Poygan for a young woman of them was with child, and so abundantly large was she her small frame appeared to teeter as she walked. They awaiting the child's arrival in a wigwam of elm bark, in this were six of them huddled, the child overdue.

"To say we took pity on them is not quite true for they were a nuisance. Teamsters complained of them taking up the road with their cluttered, straggling groups, teamsters just as soon run them over as give way. Some as foolish to set up their tea fires in the middle of the road, killed by freight wagons while tending this smug. Indian people had a thing for tea. Nothing save godless drink itself rendered them more comfort than when they did squat at the pretence of a fire, and tending with dry twigs a cantilevered tin can. They seemed capable of brewing tea from every form of vegetation. They had a tea for morning and one for mid morning, another at noon, half by noon and several with eventide. Truth was, they appeared to subsist on little else but tea in one form or another. As many were without teeth, tea was the only method available to their sustenance. All manner of leaves and bark went into their tea cans. In winter I have seen them brew tea of bird's nests and rabbit pellets, by this contrivance they survived, if meagerly.

"That this group had elected to winter over in our woods was an encumbrance for a decent person, for you could not see them and not feel pity, George and I were no different. When we told our mother of their presence she was alarmed, for while Indians were numerous enough and a common sight in summer, they were still treated with suspicion and fear. Small children were thought to disappear among them, as well as other things not nailed down. On Friday nights at the market square it was known that red robes circulated and would for a dime lie on a hayrack with a drunken farmer. If our mother resented these heathen creatures, as she called them, if she said loud and often the world would be better without them, she behaved otherwise. For when we went back to the woods with our harps on the next morning, our sleigh was burdened with what our mother called 'some old junk,' used horse blankets, tea cups without handles, a side of bacon, loaves of bread, three uncooperative hens, needles, thread, scraps of cloth, a much traveled wool coat left behind by a teamster, a pail of lard and a sack of flour. For when we mentioned of this group was a young woman with child, our mother's pity flowed. The sleigh box held also a straw tick from one of the rooms in the hotel, a cracked coffee pot, two old dresses, a pair of high-button shoes no longer in fashion, a bottle of Dr. Wolfstein's linament that looked exactly like Dr. Woodrow's linament as was for horses. A bag of green tea, another of coffee beans and some kitchen matches. It seemed as if every article in the household as was chipped, about to be thrown away, or excess, was that day transported to the Indian camp.

"George and I simply unloaded at their fire circle and went off to our day's chore of refilling the sleigh with split wood. On this we spent the day, loitered over a noontime fire with sausages and bread, napped awhile, then again to our task till the night tide. Escaping the woods in the last light, the horse followed the trail home. I was twelve, George was ten. The year was 1884, or did I say that before? The night sky was full and swollen, darkness was different in those days. It didn't merely take over, it reigned. A purring sound it made. The stars, we were told, were distant indeed, yet on these nights they seemed near, not distant at all, instead lanterns hanging just beyond us. The horse was in no hurry, and neither were we. Beneath the blanket George and I were warm and most comfortable. We, having remembered to heat several stones by our fire, now were wrapped with a sack at our feet. The heat of the stones rose and suffused our damp clothes and we were quite blissful.

"It is at such a moment that those who shall ever be farmers are born. For there is no hour more delicious than this. A thousand, ten thousand times since I have felt the same, the very same as when I was 12 years old on a sleigh making for home after a day's work. To say why this moment was so infused with joy I cannot, for the work was pitiless, and unending, and has been ever since. Yet all of it is worth this brief moment homeward. Again, I can not say why. I have in my life done the work of a dozen men. I have put my back to the plow. I have lifted a thousand potatoes by hand, shucked three thousand acres of corn, also by hand, bare-handed in November, milked cows, cleared land. From new day to dark, I did this, and all of it but to gain that bliss of going homeward at day's end.

"As the trail rose out of the woods to the high lands, the ground became firmer and easier for the horse, extending to the moraine on the east lay a broad meadow that had been cut of pine a generation before, the stumps still evident though fire had repeatedly blackened them. It was our custom in the spring to fire this meadow lest the woods take it back, with each firing the meadow more permanent. None had yet put a plow here but the stumps were to that point of decay where a good horse might roll them out. Much of what passes for land clearing is not clearing, but waiting. Wait for the mammoth roots of gigantic trees and ones not nearly so giant to rot away. Each spring, refiring the ground to hold back any regrowth. It was considered patriotic to fire a meadow, the running fire dying out on reaching the woods for they were damp and snow covered. Whether or not the land was yours, it was the duty of the passing farmer to put down a match when the conditions were right for a burn. A few days later and it might not be possible to stop the fire at the woods, the thaw being over and the understory dry enough to burn.

"At the moraine was woods again, beyond was the

field of Isaish Altenberg, veteran of the War. He who had stories to freeze the blood, stories he'd tell if no womenfolk were around. Stories of the wounds and things a person ought never see done by the most savage tribe, but were done and abundantly by church-going folk, who were head hunters in a uniform, who for want of shiny buttons were willing to perform the most hideous acts and to cover the dead with a happy tune and bright cloth.

"Emerging from the last woods we gained sight of our father's hotel, well-sited was it on a rise of ground five miles below the village. Situated on the freight route between Fort Fremont and New Berlin, the road you see was our livelihood. The light of the hotel beckoned us as it did travelers. Soon we were aware of the smell of its hospitality; the hay of the horse barn, the manure in the corral, the smell of cedar shingles and oiled harness. From the hotel came the perfumes of bread baking, laundry soap, ham in the smokehouse, stove polish, the fermentation of our father's beer cellar, a process of which he was most proud. For it had earned his innhouse a reputation of comfort not advanced by every stage stop. At two cents a glass our father believed he was making more money by his beer-making than by the hotel itself. To switch over entire and become a tavern was not however within his conscience, for we were Methodist and Methodees do not believe in libations except where they are held to be medicinal. Beer-making for purpose of hostelry and putting to sound sleep the brute and the teamster was pointedly medicinal. Our father never took drink himself, except to vouchsafe that his brew was palatable and had not oxidized, also that it was cool, had the right blend of hops, also sufficient carbonation, neither too much head nor too little, all which required tasting. For doing this, he beseeched the Lord to forgive him as it was utterly necessary. One he would not perform himself were it not to the comfort and welfare of his clients.

"To say the hotel was a welcoming sight as we emerged the woods is not accurate enough. The stone at our feet was reverting to its native temperament, we felt our hunger acutely, even the horse now hurried, smelling her own stall in the barn and warm water in the trough. That another innovation of our father, that horses and stage teams during the cold months got heated water in the trough so not to suffer cramps and binds that was then believed if a horse was given cold water. The solution was a separate winter water tank surrounded by a brick kiln and chimney that warmed the water so a worked horse could drink its fill without injury.

"How pleasant was the sight of that house in the darkness. Nothing else did signify achievement and comfort more than the lights of home. George and I quickly disengaged the sleigh at the woodpile, led the horse to the barn where it was unharnessed, watered and put to her stall, a blanket put over. We raced each other for the side door to the kitchen where we pitched off our overcoats and mittens, sopped our heads at the washboard and burst into the kitchen where supper was underway. Three extra were at the table that night besides our father, mother, sisters and brothers, as made 13 altogether. A modest number for often there were twice that number. Besides, this was Christmas Eve, and few obligations would have any other citizen abroad. With us was Dr. Taylor, a cousin, he now homeward to the village but thought to stop for a bit of supper before proceeding. He had just delivered a baby to a woman on the Stockton prairie, who turned out the child well enough without him. The other was a wild-eyed teamster by the name of Lascowski known better as the Red Rooster. His flame red hair and handle bar moustache belied his excessive spirit, he was one of the few who continued to freight regardless of the winter. Was well-known he charged double the rate and carried a barrel of lard in his box to grease the bobs in places where snow was lacking. Father was worried that Rooster had eyes for one of the sisters but would not have it as Rooster was not only Catholic, but Polish. The third guest was a frail-looking man traveling over to Jenny Bull Falls for reasons unknown. He less frail than sallow, his skin almost parchment white in comparison to the rusty hue of the Red Rooster.

"Supper on Christmas Eve was always oyster stew, which our mother served in a voluminous covered bowl of white porcelain. Oyster suppers were thought the height of sophisticated dining on the Cut-Over. Father bought several barrels of oysters in season when they could be kept iced all the way from the Chesapeake. Christmas Eve was the first supper from the barrel brought overland by Rooster the week previous.

"Like his beer, father counted on the oyster to procure revenue for the hotel by hosting such suppers throughout the winter. He charged a shilling a bowl, and two cents a glass for the beer, a fiddler at no expense, also a dance, breads, doughnuts and pickled meats for those who could not abide oysters. Though even those who thought the oyster repulsive were inclined to consume them as a prevention against goiter, a cancerous-like growth that enveloped the throat and in some cases grew to horrid excess about the neck. So routine was this disease that those who could not stomach oysters ate them anyway, hence the natural profitability of entertaining with oysters.

"Doctor Taylor was merry, as was Rooster, as was our father; our mother, being more Methodist than he, was not so merry and suspicious of the source of our father's gladness. The doctor was a round man who would in succeeding years become more so. On the rounds of his profession, he stopped at every good hostel on the way to and from another case. Was a well-known habit of his to stop midmorning at Badger when he had breakfasted only a few hours before at Plover. That he did so without charge ensured future services in the event of an ill traveler or birthing, or wounds, or horse kick or any other of the numerous accidents as might befall. It only served to make Dr. Taylor the rounder.

"George and I settled to our places at the end of the table, at a glare from our mother we bowed our heads, followed by a cursory mumble, and steaming bowls of what we privately called 'saltwater snot' were handed over.

"No sooner had we set to eating than there came a shrill cry. Everyone froze momentarily, father already rising from his place when it came again, an acute and painful cry, by this time the doctor was also on his feet. His look not so much of curiosity as consternation. George and I had already slunk from our stools, slid beneath the tablecloth and were in the cool room, reharnessed in our coats and mittens and out the door before our mother thought to admonish us lest whatever it was be something a child shouldn't see. We had long before learned if we made our escape early and without detection, our education could only benefit. The cry came again, followed by another. It issued from the barn; we running ahead, beat our father by six rods, the doctor not even close.

"In the corner of the barn behind the tackroom was a raised mow floor of oak planks. Two large doors allowed wagons to pass through the barn from one side to the other, throwing their load of hay onto the raised floor. It was a most comfortable place, the haymow, and many nights George and I had skunked over to the barn, spending the night there rather than in the overcrowded and noisy hotel.

"There in the corner of the haymow was the Indian from the marsh woods and his now suffering wife whose splayed legs were obvious. George and I had seen many a baby born, if not yet a human child. Doctor Taylor arrived out of breath as might be expected, in a few seconds he appraised the situation, sent George for two buckets of warm water and a cake of soap while I was to fetch a lantern. *'Two if you please,'* he shouted after, *'and see the chimneys are clean.'* I ran to the forge house where my father had a row of spare lanterns set by for emergency. Miscellaneous lanterns he had traded and swapped for, holed ones which he soldered up to hold oil, rewicked and filled with oil, several dozen of them hanging in a row above the forge room. Ready, lest a horse go down on the road after dark, ready to replace any of the hundred at the hotel. We had lanterns for the root cellar, lanterns for the outhouse, lanterns for the cold room, the tackroom, the laundry, the smokehouse, the barrel room, the tater cellar. Pa hung lanterns on wires after dark where the stage was to stop. If a stage was overdue we lit up the lanterns so the moment they surmounted the last moraine they could see our light and make for it. There was, he said, good business in that. On oyster nights Pa put out a dozen lanterns on both sides of the road, quite extravagant was this, with oil at five cents a gallon.

"The Indian woman was at hard labor, her man apologetic, saying it was their intent to get home to the woods for having the child but her moment arrived. They had been to the village for salt, thread and gunpowder, on the return her water broke, despite their haste the child proved insistant. He again apologized to Pa for stealing room in the barn but the need was immediate and they would leave soon as the child was dry.

"Pa, who had no high opinion of Indians, was a good man, said they could stay as they needed. Doc Taylor scolded Pa with a look, saying he'd have none of that, soon as the child was born they were to have his room in the hotel and he would spend the night in the barn. This raised Pa's fur but it settled soon enough 'cause he knew that Indians wouldn't do that, instead be gone by the first light, making the last miles to their woods being they didn't know how to rightly use a bed, whether to sleep on it or under it.

"In the light of a lantern that night I saw a child born. It came the same way a calf comes, slimy, wrinkled and steaming. Then it's lungs fill, the kid bellows and what was pasty and clay-colored tinted like dawn itself. Neither George nor I had seen that before.

"By morning they were gone. It was snowing. It was also Christmas, which meant ham and suet pudding for dinner, and licorice and hard candy. My mama never did have a tree in her house. When I married a Lutheran, I agreed as part of the deal to take up a tree at Christmas. Never mind my mother thought my soul was forfeit. My brother George was the same, he married George Tragasser's dark daughter, the school marm. They took up with the tree 'cause of her being Episcopalian and very nearly a Catholic. If it hadn't been for the Lutherans and Catholics we wouldn't have a Christmas tree yet.

"I remember it snowing, or did I already say that? Cold too, but somehow I don't remember that as well; is the snow I remember. A lazy, still-air snow, a crystal ball sort of snow. My job was to feed and water the horses. George had the chicken coop to tend, after breakfast lime down the outhouse and put fire in the laundry.

"My barn chores done, I happened to look on the place where the baby was born. The hay was flattened out and cold, meaning they had left some while before. In the place of them was this stone."

At this, great chewed-over, knotted-up, bitten-off, dog-eared Uncle Jim opened his hand and revealed the stone. It was less stone that it was jewel, a gem the same color as dawn coming on the world. The same color as new breath in a baby.

"This," Uncle Jim said, "the very stone. If you look close you can see the skyline, the way it is all dark and mournful, then dawn happens, the color rises, and it is day again."

Great Uncle passed the stone from his hand, his warmth still in it. When it had made the circle of us Uncle Jim returned it to a leather pouch, sized to fit that tiny arrowhead, this he slipped back into his pocket.

It was George's turn.

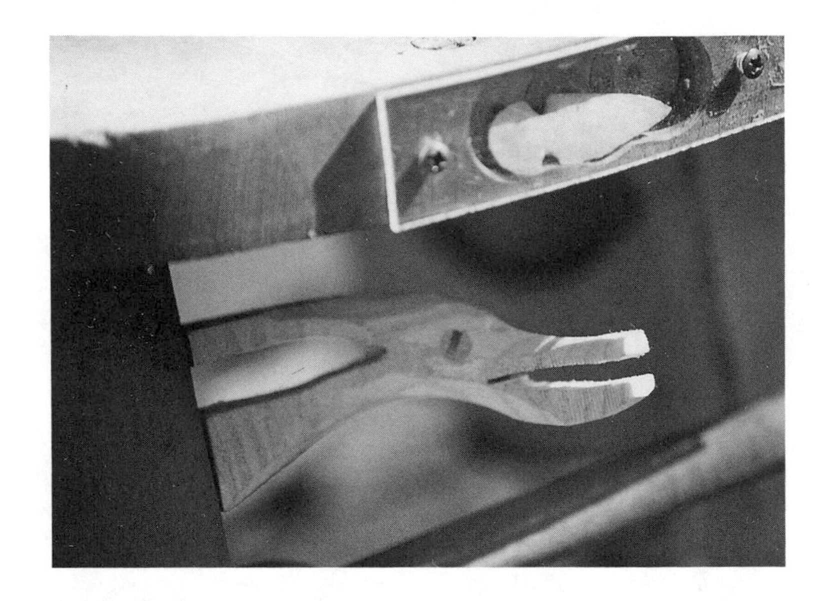

A Lesson in Beasts

1953. The last story told by George had been a failure, in fact some worse than a failure. The story he related had involved an orphan, a limp and a lost dog; it was a prime-time, made-for-television story where nothing got killed, squashed or event pinched a finger. Nobody died, not even the Christmas goose because they were all vegetarians. Worse yet they were from Minnesota where they don't even eat soybeans 'cause an angleworm might die before the plough. As said, an exceeding failure, and this my own grandfather. Such a very bad story was it that my mama applauded.

In 1953 George told his last stone story. The following April he was dead. A person can tell some things, like if it's gonna rain six inches all at one darn once versus drizzle half an inch. Not as there is a regular sort of stick to go by, but it is measureable just the same. So is going. We all knew George, the grandfather, was going. There was a storm cloud over him, the rounded off sort of cloud that hang low and wounded, the air of a sudden colder. The winds still and about to get terrible, same as grandfather was sometimes still and then terrible, like he was gonna die.

Then he did die. We put him in a box, to look at awhile, afterwards we buried him at Yellow Banks, not far from where Charlie the MacGregor Rice had his hotel and his great lum. Buried him on an April morning, it was about noon, the rhubarb was up and everybody came to the house for tea and sandwiches. All the uncles were there, all the aunts, his brothers who were teetering some themselves smoked cigars in his honor, White Owls they were.

But none of that had happened yet for this was the Christmas before, when George told his last stone. As said, we knew it as his last, least the odds were favorable because of his weather signs.

The thing about George was he believed quite the opposite as an adult is supposed to. Was George who taught me how to smoke a pipe; I was six. Don't inhale, not tamp it too tight, once a day, same as prayer. Taught me how to smoke cigars, too. Sunday only, if maybe on Saturday afternoon but then you skip Sunday. Read one thing a day, write one thing a day, drink tea for good health, study birds, also clouds, plant trees, listen to opera. Do not inhale. My grandfather believed the opposite as is the wont of psychologists to believe, that an early and vigorous helping of scary is a favor to a child. Which explains his lesson in beasts.

At this last Christmas George told his last stone, he knew it to be his last, which explains why he gave it away. Did I ever mention that my grandfather was not particularly generous? When he let me smoke his cigar it was always the stump, the slimy, wet stump; as said, not real generous.

Was that Christmas, 1953 he told of the dragon, how it was the obligation of every good person when they are of capable age to go to the woods and find their very dragon. *'Nathair sgiathach,'* he said. (na'hain sgihock). He told us to select a quality dragon and not a cheap imported model because a dragon like a wife, it is for life. I immediately countered, as well I should, that we were much too young to make a decision like this, that perhaps he'd better come along, if not he maybe our mother.

My grandfather did not get stern very often.

"*'Your mother will not go with 'e to find your dragon. You will either go alone or you will not go. If you whimper you are not ready.'*"

I was cured of my fear, least most of it.

"*'So where,'* I asked grandfather, *'where is it that dragons live? How shall we know the dragon sign? Do they poop?'*"

"*'Green poop,'* said he. *'Easily confused with lichen that covers the forest floor, is no else but dragon poop.'*"

Apparently I had seen dragon poop all along.

My grandfather could tell we were apprehensive. He beckoned us to come closer and never mind the smell of his cigar. Then he spoke into our ears like he was passing a secret, though it was less said than spat.

"*'I'll give ye the stane,'* said 'e. Digging from his pocket a small stone that appeared innocent and not at all the stone to protect us from the depredations of a grouchy dragon who'd as soon eat us as pass the time of day.

I knew, we knew, the stone was a complete fraud. Grandfather was about tell how if I had this stone in my pocket no dragon would do me harm. The same as when the Sunday School teacher said wearing a cross next to my skin did protect me from sin and death. In all likelihood untrue, but calming. I took the stone.

As I chanced to turn over the pebble, I saw smack in the middle was a hole. Now everyone knows a hole in a stone is unlikely.

He saw my eyebrows rise. "*'I see you thought this an ordinary stone and not the dragon-keeper as I told. You thought I was running on as is the old man thing, and this another mythology to tend children in ways known to keep them tame.'*"

I was astonished.

"*'I'll have you know this is a rare stone. Given me by my ain grandda in 1888, to him by heen in 1840 and the himen before in 1799, and so on from George and Fergus and Daniel and Angus and Donald, all of them in a line as goes back three thousand years, from pocket to pocket it went, put in the charge of small boys, who had been chosen to tend the stane, the dragon and the woods. The family has always had its stone, its dragon and the woods.*

"*'Unlike the fool English we do not kill our dragons. We do not invite slayers with bright swords to prick our dragon's heart. We do not set up smudges in the eveningtide to darken the sky to shy them off. We do not burn their lairs, not kill their green children, instead we . . .'* at this point my grandfather leaned over to my ear and he whispered heavily into it '*. . . instead we keep them.*' "

" '*Dragons?*' I asked.

" '*Aye, dragons. Now it is your turn.*' "

He handed me the stone that was on one side plain and ordinary and on the other porous and rare. I was skeptical. A fool trick this, of the old rimers and cripples, of way too many poets of the semi-employed kind. Three millenia thick of their conniving, this horrid business about dragons, for no other reason than to see a child made the fool. A cruel trick as any can see. Yet was that hole. A curious hole. A most unreasonable hole. I was disbelieving, but not entirely. Grandfather went on.

" '*I read your thoughts. You think what an honest child ought, that this is all hocus pocus and you are being fluffed. I can not tell you otherwise, fact is I have never seen a dragon and that business about dragon poop . . . well, I made that up, seemed a right thing to say, to . . . to . . . convince you. Was no different with my grandman. You should have heard the story he smoked, had me believing in gilt-winged dragons who slept among the roots of giant trees with emerald acorns. There were, said 'e, lair trees. I believed. On rainy afternoons I went looking for evidence of them, feathers or scales or whatever dragons have.*' "

Grandfather could read my question . . . '*And?*'

" '*Nay dragons. Not once ever did I see the beast or its poop. I did entertain that every lightning strike was their sign. And the evening fog as gathers in the low fields was the breath of them, and a pileated hole was where they stored their young. I fabricated quite a glossary of their habits and plumage. I knew how they tended their young, and their favorite recipes. In the end I had to admit I was deceiving myself. Later I scared my own children with dragon stories, causing them lie quiet in their beds. How they hugged the covers with their eyes hanging out like new risen moons; I laughed. Eventually they also learned it wasn't true; didn't matter, they went on to scare their children just the same. They too held the bed clothes tight round them and did not go berrying till they were old and wise enough to do battle with their fear as had become monumental.'"*

'"So, it's all a bleeding hoax, is it?'"

"'Hoax? don't be such a dunce, boy. Listen to what I'm saying. You are the stone man now. It is not for you to keep dragons as for you to keep the place of dragons. For a family without stories, without bairns hugging the covers, without granddads and grandmams waxing sordid tales about fabulous beasts and telling what discomforting things were done to Great Auntie Bernice as was gobbled whole when she wandered off. Without the words to connect us, what's the power of blood? Now it's your problem, you are the stane-keeper.'"

This, what my grandfather said, at his last Christmas, his last stone, when I was a wee bairn.

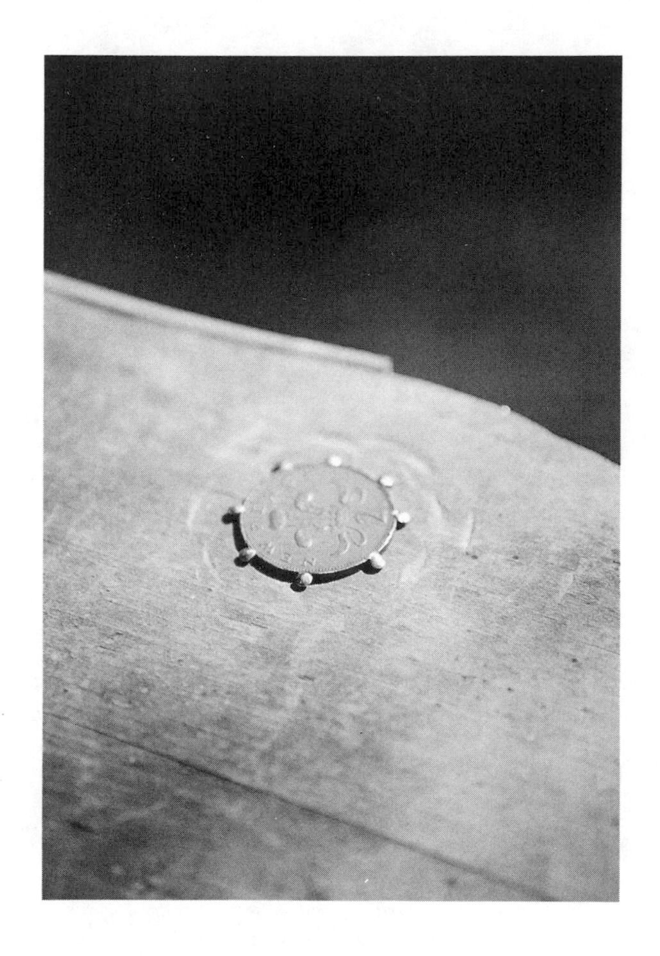

There Appeared a Host, Singing

Demanding. Christmas is too demanding. The chief implement of a Christmas story is the premeditated lie, but you already know that. It is a durable tradition, one even the most hardy storyteller must uphold. This is the dilema of Christmas, for Christmas is too demanding . . . too sumptuous . . . to render plain and undecorated. That the uncles maintained brave fact and inviolate truth in every other endeavor; Christmas did release their conscience from the standard of society and of Methodists, that they might then become purveyors of the the transcending and spectacular lie.

That my family tolerated this was for want of mirth, this the alliance of those devoted to Methodism, a vacancy we felt seasonally compelled to augment. Kindled within an otherwise antiseptic farm kind that is for good reason godly and smug, but briefly, willingly surrender to the intoxicating story, that transforming spirit as was in the stone.

It was not that Uncle Henry was weird. That we already knew, for 'E, Uncle Henry, had by his own conscience deserted the family, married a damnable southern sort, and moved blanket and duffel to a bloodthirsty region. 'E who was about to tell a stone. It was Uncle 'E who told the story of the corn Indians, and turned my mama white, she white enough in the first place. Uncle Henry turned her some whiter with his story as wasn't very Christmasy. He the Uncle gaining the chair, sittin', clearing his throat the way old people do, like they just swallowed an entire muskrat and now want to cough up the left-over fur and bones.

"This story suffers numerous lies, but they are truthful lies intended for the betterment of the human. The scene is real enough, an' you can go see it for yourself if you want. I will take certain liberties with the site for by its own it is a little known village.

"My story is about Keene . . . Keene, Wisconsin and what happened there in 1936. A smart village was Keene, having a tavern, hardware, post office, bakery, gas station, shoe repair, health clinic and various other services including a paralegal. They were, though, all served by the self-same enterprise, this the Keene Tavern, located on the south berm of the bridge crossing of a length of trout-prone water.

"'The Keene,' as they called it, was the central reservoir of needs as were brought to it, both human and mechanical. Each stumbled away some better chewed if not exactly resolved. Be it wingnut, a dozen corks, writing paper, sandpaper, flypaper, toilet paper; the essentials of life, and assorted venal sins, were to be had from this one source. Stamps, chicken wire, baking soda, flour, breath mints, eight penny nails, .30 caliber bullets and that more fitting squirrels, jackknives, pencils, sympathy cards, chocolates, Dr. Penwarren's Famous Bag Balm and a miscellany of other repairs and dotages. Nothing on earth deserving to remain in one piece in the first place failed to find repair, or at least consolation, at 'The Keene.'

"The clapboard tavern sat center of what natives call 'The Wash,' a narrow profile allowing passage from the glaciated hills on the east to the flatland on the west. The road furtively darting through the gap in the moraine as if to do so before greater geology thought better of the lapse and took it back. That Keene existed was due to this sincere freak of nature, a small gap in the hills that should'na by the routines of charity owned such a convenience.

"West of Keene lay the moor long known as the Buena Vista, an environ not satistfied to be merely reluctant to agriculture. Few other conditions of earth have spit out innocent pilgrims as quick, as remorselessly as the marsh. On appearance the soil resembled Iowa, so fertile, so sweet a farmer might eat it by the mouthful and thrive. Its victims did not recognize the pretense; the marsh was nothing but a degenerate swamp whose rancid soil couldn't raise parsnips next to the outhouse.

"For years waves of emigrants came, strived awhile, then succumbed to this fool's earth. The stubborn endured, farming the high spots while compromising their holdings with fields in the broad morainal valley beyond 'The Wash,' a soil comprised of erratics and till, meaning rocks. A farmer with two different planets at his disposal might just contrive a living for his effort, this how Keene came to be.

"That Keene had all the attributes of decency, save a church, was well-known to its inhabitants. While the schoolhouse served also the Sunday meeting, it lacked the distinctive prejudice of a kirkhouse, and at no time was this more evident than at Christmas. The carols, the implausible story of St. Luke, require the tending of a kirk to exact the proper effect; God's word without His tabernacle is deprived a central mystery.

"The Methodist ministry tending Keene had on numerous occasions attempted fund drives to implement church construction, a call that fell on deaf ears and deafer wallets, times being hard and worse, what with the proximity of the marsh. What bothered the attending seminarian was the farmers of his flock owned a fair and gleaming array of agricultural progress, yet they could not, or would not, supplement the building fund. Three parishoners even had tractors, whose sum total value equaled a cathedral complete with bell, gothic window and a three-story pulpit. Every theology student knows it is a shoddy gospel lesson to preach great Moses from a school desk, much less have George Washington looking over your shoulder.

"This stalemate continued until the conference serving Keene inferred the lack of enthusiasm represented a corresponding faithlessness. The presiding minister regretfully announced, from the school desk, that services at Keene were to end with Christmas Eve, as the conference could no longer tolerate the lack of an honest steeple.

"The congregation was knocked in a tizzy by the news. While they heard the threat previously, they had no thought the heirarchy might abandon them. Baptists wouldn't do such a thing, Lootrans neither, and not on your life would Catholics vacate a parish as long as one believer remained. As a result the farmers of Keene were both challenged and insulted, a dangerous combination.

"Farmers, as most everyone knows, are peculiar about religion. How a ploughman prays is different from the method advertized in the manual. There is a kind of prayer at milking, as the forehead lies against the comforting flank of the beast. There is the specialized prayer at plough handles. And prayer at planting, and prayer at dawn. Prayers for the failed, the bleeding, the dead and those things near about dead. Prayers for withered crops and slaughter-bound cows. This still moment when a farmer lays his petition before eternity, the Big E itself. Agriculture is awful enough; without a proximal deity, it is beyond endurance.

"The Methodist lay leaders held their monthly at The Keene over root beer and peanuts, the announced end of worship services their concern. Attending were Johnson, Eckels, MacQuarrie and Ted Bannach, who despite being Catholic regularly attended the meetings.

"'Not much you can do then ?'

"'The Conference says we're to have construction in hand else services shall cease.'

"'Myself, I don't see what is so blame short with

the schoolhouse. It's empty on Sunday anyhow. Why all the lather ?'

"*'Cause it don't look like a kirk and that counts for some. It's a cat but it ain't calico.'*

"*'Well, I guess that's the end of the dog's tail. We'll either be going to Liberty Corners or go without.'*

"*'Yep, guess, so.'*

"*'You could move the old kirk, you know.'* Was Ted Bannach as said it.

"*'What ?'*

"*'The kirk up on the hill spared by the tornado '91. . . old man Guth kept apples in it but now he's got a ground cellar it's empty . . . you could move it.'*

"*' I didn't know it was a kirk. How d'you know ?'*

"*'Cause that's the story.'*

"*'That don't make it one.'*

"*' Well . . .There's a pulpit in it, big ol' butternut jack-o-lantern thing higher up than a peel tower.'*

"*'Move it ?'*

"*'Lock, stock and peanut shell.'*

"*'You think so ?'*

"*'Course I think so. We've tractors enough to tow the pharoah's tomb much less that bit of church.'*

"Thus the plot was hatched. On no more than root beer it was hatched, and with it a new zeal for tractors. Farmers, sensing a new power to them, feeling in their very souls the pull of their Cases, Fordsons and McCormick-Deerings, at ten, even, can you imagine, twelve horsepower each. 'Course they could move a kirk.

"For this community of farmers, the Christmas program was the high point of their cosmopolitan year. It filled their untended and vacant hearts, it called them to light and joy. Together they'd join the tune, ' . . . God rest ye merry gentlemen, let nothing you dismay . . .' The ragged carol uprooted from their untilled hearts and sent twinkling among the hills, casting a fragile armistice over the cruel moor. The tune, the candles, the gentle hush of the snow, together softened the harsh farm reality into something almost . . . picturesque.

"Every year did this gentle parish enact the natal pageant. A rustic affair, farmers and hired men became the shepherds and wisemen, costumed in borrowed bathrobe with a foil-wrapped crown for Caesar Augustus. A pathetic stagecraft it was, the mumbled lines, ill-advised costumes, but secreted in each participant was the rare innoculation of that story. That ever-so-rare, if not altogether risky attempt to find the holy. The girl who played Mary wondered how she'd know if God touched her. Would it come as a breeze or would she hear voices? Did God have fingers? At the annual Christmas pageant there were farmers who asked primitive questions no right-thinking seminarian would dare. Thus was a measure of holiness gained, at least enough for this place.

"The difficulty of moving a thirty by fifty building one half mile was not entirely discounted by the incredible, enormous, tumultuous, exaltant . . . if not ungodly horsepower of tractors. Imagine, twelve horsepower out of a single cantankerousness. The problem wasn't the weight of the old kirk, wasn't the coefficient of the drag, or the strength of the tow chain. The problem was downhill. The empty kirk stood at the brow of the moraine and the next two hundred yards were at a grade known to be self-perpetuating. It was apparent to everyone that once edged beyond the brow, once in motion, the structure soon after would overtake the tractors and arrive at the valley floor well before them. Not at all the desired effect. What they needed was a series of pulleys and belays not only to get the structure started downhill, but then to moderate its natural inclinations for the headlong flight.

"Estimates vary; some renditions of the story say a multitude showed up the Wednesday morning they moved the church off the hill. That count was inflated. If a hundred attended, it was every man, woman and child in the township including the Catholic parish who turned out not so much to advance the Methodist cause as bear witness to the glory of tractors. Some say twenty-seven paraffin-fueled tractors were present and one Rumley. The stouter kids were deployed to lug the rolling stock, to set, then reset it under the timber carriage; other kids, less stout, were to advance the planks. Quite a pageant ensued. There were tractors smokin', the ground was dug up, men grunting, engine misfires, kids sliding downhill, babies bawling, the steam engine belching a coal-scented cloud, whistles, yelling, the joyless chime of logging chain. The steamer, being near equal the weight of the kirk, was at the bottom of the hill attached to the belay, the rope wetted and sent uphill, snaked around an oak tree, this in order to prevent that building from overtaking the tractors. Least that was the theory.

"Few spectacles this side of semi-naked archangels can call up farmers more enthusiastically than tractors. The town's entire census was gathered on the hill. Womenfolk, being the more fragile when it comes to sparks and loud noises, stood back from the event and were the more comfortable. They had a fire going and a coffee pot, fresh doughnuts and bandages. Bandages necessary, 'cause wouldn't be any fun if someone didn't get hurt.

"Three hours and eighteen minutes exactly it took to tip the kirk off the hill and lug it overland to the vacancy behind The Keene. Where it was jacked up, the skids removed, the sill plate set on sandstone, steps improvised, chimney installed, and the stove refit. In less than five hours the job was complete; one half mile, one down-hill, one bridge crossing . . . one small kirk reset. The menfolk and their tractors retired to evening chores, and this the very day of Christmas Eve.

"The story ought to end here, the honest one would do so. The scene as described is Christmasy enough. What more can be wanted? A church has been moved by good will, human effort and a little ingenuity, the dominion of tractors was observed and exalted, some religions of the world were gathered to one purpose, the host was served by doughnut, the consecrated wine deposed by undilute coffee. Methodists were seen to lay down, or at least sit down, with Catholics and Lutherans, for an earnest pull and loud hosannah of tractors. It was a good time if not a very good time and no one had yet spent a prayer to make it better. It was holy enough. The kirk was moved. The Rumley Steamer was put back in its shed, the tractors also bedded down, radiators drained, blankets put over. The story really should end here. Any who is still loitering about waiting for a miracle to occur are bound for disappointment. What was told is true, the kirk at Keene was moved, by tractors, and on Christmas Eve. That is the story. It is done, done without customary Christmas breach of scientific credibility. Done with a tractor which, for a farm-type community, is a nice touch. The story has a comfort and like said, is true enough, yet it lacks sentiment. It is this tradition of the Chrismas telling that bids me to continue in hope that some weakness in the narrative can be exploited.

"When the congregation returned for the evening service, the kirk was no longer the former apple shed of the Guths, it was dark and hollow no longer. It was quite otherwise. Candles and kerosene lamps were arrayed on every cornice and step, a more evocative scene being hard to imagine. This wee kirk posed most romantically against the dark winter scene of The Wash, at Keene, Wisconsin, 1936.

"The seminarian to Keene, being city-born, did not know the difference between tractor miracles and the other kind. He was an unmechanical man. The very type as are disposed to take up the word of God because they can not fix or build anything on earth, so they might as well be deployed to the repair of the kingdom of Heaven. That evening as he approached The Wash on his way to what he knew in fact as the last worship service, he was a man in danger of losing his creed. For among Methodists the act of miracles is unnecessary. Miracles were thus not to be advanced nor admired. But there before him, at the junction of two country roads, stood now a church where none existed before. Around it were parked more vehicles than he had ever known to attend one of his services, funerals included. He spied the yellow DeSoto of a known

Baptist, the rumble seat coupe of a devout Catholic and the false-floor Model A of the town's premier moonshiner. Easily a hundred strong were here to attend his service, twice, three, ten times the norm. In the low light of kerosene and candles it resembled a most biblical multitude. There were people standing in the aisles, jammed in the vestibule, kids sitting Indian-style at the rostrum.

"That night when he read from the second chapter of Luke's affidavit, '*. . . and it came to pass in those days,*' the gospel of the possible woke in him as it had never before, he felt the Nativity as he never would again. The carols wrapped a swaddling cloth around all those who were there . . . it came upon a midnight clear . . . and it had indeed.

"Again my story is at conclusion. I should know better than to go on, for is not the conclusion here comfortable enough? I really should leave it and turn the story chair to another. But, I shall not.

"The Methodist congregation at Keene for reason of dwindling numbers and the farm ecomony did close six years later. Those who remained joined with Liberty Corners at the onset of the Second World War. The seminarian enlisted and spent the length of his service writing letters of regret to next of kin above the signature of General Eisenhower. The tornado of '46 took the roof off the deserted church, the remnants were dismantled to favor a chicken coop. A cabbage patch now resides where it once stood. In 1955 'The Keene' closed for business to the dismay of local farmers who were certain this was the sign of the apocolypse being upon them. The burr oak tree at the head of the moraine, whose barrel was greased to the rope as let the kirk down the hill was still there. Now grown hollow. The only time the Catholics and Methoders meet now is over chicken and biscuit at their annual fall suppers, leading one to think theology is better left in the care of Betty Crocker and Aunt Jemima if it's bread-breaking power you're after.

"The seminarian never did comprehend how the kirk was moved but kept the miraculous nature of its appearance to himself lest it offend his theology. As said, he was most unmechanical, it just a matter of rope enough, some planks, some pulp logs, despite in his mind it was the same caliber as performed by Moses at the Red Sea. Methodists aren't supposed to believe in miracles just because they don't understand how a thing happened. If they did, Cyrus McCormick would wind up a saint and you can't very well have that, though I don't see why not. Still, when it comes to miracles, some things is and some things isn't."

Uncle Henry put his hands across his chest, confident of his story doing all what a decent Christmas story should. It told the truth, and only when attempting to comply with the public addiction did it wander off. However it did not satisfy his wife, who was the female (Confederate) from Missouri, further blemished by being Irish, and as such addicted to elves, angels and levitations. In her opinion a Christmas story as does not end in a good, wet cry isn't Christmasy enough.

Children often have better literary sense than females and had they been consulted, Uncle Henry might have adjourned, but he had his darling to satisfy. She being not the least bit effected by the tractors, which shows how far off peculiar she was.

Uncle Henry of St. Louis, removed his hands from his chest, place them on his knees, took a deep breath and did continue.

"Keene was the second municipality to occupy The Wash, the first village was located a few hundred rods upstream. A fragrant little enterprise was that of Buena Vista, having a complete set of hospitalities; hotel, three saloons, grist mill, lumber mill, dance hall, chance hall, a loose women's guild and a livery. A veritable metropolis. But Buena Vista was something other than a timid innocent village enjoying the sawdust flavor of the Old Pinery. Buena Vista existed by chance and for chance; in particular, poker, dice and a weighted wheel. In the days of pine, no wilder, no more entertaining resort existed in this northern clime than was the allure of the village of Buena Vista. It possessed the necessary amenities; here the tourist could lose his shirt, step out of his trousers and shoe the horse, all at the same franchise. The liquor, though homemade and watered, was cheap, the ladies were experienced and the bedclothes washed the first of the month. A village with an industrial-grade ambition like this can't help but thrive and Buena Vista would today be a city of 40,000 had it not been for the whallop of '91. In 1891 God the Almighty Smoke himself reached down and smashed Buena Vista to bits. Everybody knew God done it 'cause nobody else can steer a tornado. Smack through Buena Vista it went, destroying everything. Not an outhouse, pigsty or bluebird house was left standing . . . flat dab smashed was the village of cut card and perfumed chemise. Everything wrecked and scattered . . . except for . . . the kirkhouse of Reverend Alex Kolloch. Not even the window panes were broken. That as clear a demonstration of God-sent brimstone and heck as you can ever hope to witness.

"Though the site was promising the village was not rebuilt. Popple and scrub oak grew among the wreckage, the streets and alleys were returned to the squirrel woods and most people forgot there ever was a village of Buena Vista.

"How there came to be a kirk in this den of iniquity is pertinent to our continuing search for a satisfying Christmas story.

"Alexander Kolloch is the ancestor to the pioneer family whose subsequent ventures have enjoyed remarkable success. By his first choice Alexander was not a man of the cloth, fully the opposite; a rough, bare-knuckled woods-jack was he. He had hands the size of watermelons and a tongue capable of smoldering an oath two rods wide and filling in gopher holes as it went.

"In 1861 he, with a tangle of other pine boys, signed on with Col. Alban's 18th Wisconsin to shuck the South of their recalcitrant error. A simple adventure it was in the abstract, especially with the enlistment bonus paid upfront.

"Every school child now knows of the protracted civil meanness that had befallen the nation, one of whose chapters was saved for the Alban Regiment. On a Sunday morning of 1861, Alexander found himself pinned face-down in the dirt by rifle fire thicker than mayflies, bullets nipping off grass a goat wouldn't eat. Alexander did then what any sane person might in the circumstance. He made a hasty but solemn pact with God. If the Lord of Heaven would by His majesty, and if He pleased, at His earliest opportunity, might, if He wan't overbusy, extract Alexander from this carnage and certain death, then Alexander would take up the Lord's cause the rest of his living days. God, as everyone knows, is a humorist.

"Alexander survived that awful morning at Pittsburg Landing, a little after he had prayed for his salvation he was taken prisoner, from then until the war's conclusion a guest of Andersonville prison. Being a simple man and good to his word, Alexander Kolloch did not recognize he had been cheated by God, who had saved his life but unconscionably so. In Andersonville, Kolloch began his ministry, three years later he emerged an 87 pound dynamo of the gospel having witnessed more insanity, cruelty and deprivation than intellect can tolerate without resort to antidote.

"In 1868 he retuned to Buena Vista and began holding services behind the clothesline of the Chinese laundry; they were sparsely attended. He started the construction of a small church, cutting down and hauling the logs himself. In Buena Vista he enjoyed the celebrated prerogatives of the ministry; the borrowed horse, the loaned wagon, the sawyers day off in exchange for funeral services and what various other ceremonies spiritual intercession improves. Reverend Kolloch with his diverse education in the ways of God had a willingness to bless and sanctify what other catechisms might not. He ministered to drunks, gamblers, whores, foul-breathed teamsters and muck farmers. He refereed the Friday night pugilism, once served communion using a loaf of sourdough bread and moraine-born whiskey. Was the kirk of Alexander Kolloch that God left behind when the tornado of '91 smashed the village of Buena Vista. The good Reverend died with everyone else that day, way too smart to ask God to spare him again. Buried without ceremony with the girls, the gamblers, and the river dogs somewhere on the backside of the moraine in a common grave."

Uncle Henry's wife still wasn't crying. Suggesting the elements of the story are yet too spartan, how they sorta dodge, she thinks intentionally, the heartstrings instead of plucking deliberately at them. Maybe, she says to be instructive, it's the mention of the whores, the drunks and the whiskey. She believes a retelling is in order, but Uncle Henry has grown weary and thinks the story already excessive. Perhaps he could say something about Alexander's grave. But that won't do any good, since as said, it was a common hole. Same appliance shared with his last companions, who were professionals themselves, they all buried up on the moraine, at the bluff line, if a little west of it, overlooking a pretty un-remarkable stretch of marshland. Not the sort of prospect liable to encounter adoration.

Uncle Henry knew how it was; people, mostly though it was females, want a little epiphany with their conclusion no matter how raw and obnoxious the attachment. Sometimes, if far more rare, farmers want a little moral flourish to finish off a story. Farmers who aren't otherwise addicted to such poetics, but just once in awhile want to see it done for the sake of the mechanism, to know it ain't rusted. An old-fashioned sentiment and likely to be . . . well . . . untrue, still, there is such a thing as a good end. Uncle Henry gently continued.

"Some there are who say the wind in that squirrel woods above The Wash has sounds likened to those that bullets make. The clear low whistle of bullets at a close pass. Like those heard the morning of Alban's regiment. Some say this woods on the moraine has this most particular sound, the like of which is not heard in any other woods. Others say the sound is of a wet rope snaking round a greased oak tree. Others, more imaginative and hopeful, hear silk. Some think it the steam hiss of an over-worked 10-20 McCormick Deering.

"Some there are who think the woods above Keene are ghosted. I have stood on that hill myself in the early darkness. To the east rumble the townships of stone and rock; west, the wide flat of the black and ungrateful moor. I have stood there on a winter night, following the trail of others who have also come and stood. Come to listen, listen to this peculiar woods.

"The wind, as I hear it, says what angels might if angels could. Maybe it is just the pines there as say it. I have thought too, maybe it is the ghost of Alexander who has yet that promise to keep. Alexander, though dead and long since rendered to dust and earth, yet keeps to his oath. He preaching forever after the ways of peace. That is, my darlings, why the wind on the moraine over Keene calls out the name . . . Shiloh."

Uncle 'E shut off then, but not before reaching into his pocket and extracting from it a watch chain. To it was attached an object we did not at first recognize, for it resembled a round pebble, a very round pebble.

Puzzled, we looked at Uncle 'E. And he in a hushed, barely audible voice, whispered . . . "Shiloh."

Epilogue

And it came to pass they were no more. One by one they faded and died. They couldn't make it to Christmas, their hearts were bad, the rheumatism flared up, sometimes they were just old. Uncle Ed died, they buried him with his Stetson on his chest. Before they closed the lid they fit it to his head. All his life he feared colds and pneumonia from being caught bareheaded. Uncle Ed, when he bathed, did so with a hat on.

George died and Henry and Uncle Jesse who smoked handrolls. A couple of kitchen matches were secreted in his pocket in case he went to heaven, where a dry match is hard to find.

Christmas seemed vacant without them, without the bickering of the brothers, without the dreadnaughts who were aunts and thought to better the noise of the boys, without the potato-cellar smell of Uncle Ed, without Uncle Henry and his glass bottle of termites.

They died one by one until only Uncle Jim remained, Uncle Jim who yet farmed with horses, who spent his summer fixing fence, a bent over man who tended the strands, his pockets hazardous with staples, his mushed-face hammer, clucking to his horses: then he too died.

Christmas did not go away but it was a different animal. It belonged more to Lionel and Mattel, a must-have was the Lone Ranger double holster set complete with a badge and chrome-plated six shooters that stopped evil right smack in its tracks with a silver bullet through a black and deserving heart. Christmas was Bing Crosby and Perry Como, even the Kingston Trio had a holiday album, and suddenly and irrevocably Christmas was stuff, stuff by the ton and megaton. It was Nike and Commodore, and those noisome little devices that children beat with buttons causing them to sit glass-eyed in one spot, immobilized, trying to devour something.

Was Dorothy who started it again, the mother-in-law. One year Dorothy told a story on Christmas; it was not a very good story, it lacked action, it was too calm and had not a single precipice, not even a sharp stick, it was cozy and not very truthful. Instead it possessed all the right and good motives that people are generally not. It was dressed-up and gussied, it was too rich, too sugary, and not very digestable . . . but it was a story.

Dorothy told this story on Christmas Eve with the family fathered round. Nothing exploded, it had no wolves, nothing caught fire, no blood was spilled, everybody got home safely. In fact it was an awful story, a sorry-ass story that took place somewhere in Illinois near

Peoria where now is the Caterpillar plant. The parking lot of Caterpillar Corporation in 1858, was a homestead with a log cabin and a quilt. The quilt was a blue and white percale in the Morning Star pattern stuffed with milkweed, but the story lacked Indians, tomahawks and knives.

There wasn't anybody who heard that story who didn't think they could tell a better one than Dorothy.

Every year when the family meets for Christmas, we gather for the consumption of an enormous well-browned victim. There is stuffing and mashed potatoes . . . I do not allow my mother-in-law to touch the potatoes because she does not know how to mash them properly, she does not use enough milk, she does not beat them sufficiently. Mashed potatoes done right are airy and liable to float off same as a dirigible; they do not set up on the plate like my mother-in-law's mashed potatoes, very akin to mortar mix.

After the supper we exchange gifts. There is a standing war between the brothers-in-law, to give weird and horrid things for Christmas, a ployester day-glo pink tie and the most god-awful ugly socks, ball point pens with ladies in them who undress when the pen gets warm, a set of discount store markers baked in an oven so the ink will never flow. One year I gave brother-in-law Dan an adjustable wrench securely welded into a piece of pipe, believing it would take him a week to pry it open. With a cold chisel he had it open the next morning before breakfast, the noise of his hammer heard at a most uncivilized hour.

After the necessary exchange of treaty items, we tell stories because Dorothy started it. Some are maudlin and gushy, some are true, some straight from the Bible, some few are invented. Stories told about threshing in 1932 and planting ten acres of potatoes by hand. About winters when it snowed a lot more than it does now, about losing the farm to the river in Illinois, about Iwo Jima and the Battle of the Bulge, about a swamp in central Wisconsin where an old canoe maker yet dwells who peels birch bark and makes of it canoes that sell in town for $2,000 each. The guy is plumb beautiful crazy. Stories of the merchant marine and north Atlantic, stories of one-room schools, of she who was once a riveter for Lockheed and saw the Richard Bong himself.

The stones, it seems, are still talking.

Epilogue

PHOTO BY MARY "CASEY" MARTIN

ABOUT THE AUTHOR

JUSTIN ISHERWOOD is a farmer on that episode of sand known to inhabit the central region of Wisconsin. His family has been equated with the place since the 1830's, farmers mostly, perpetually bordering on extinction as is the known method of the agricult.

Potatoes, green beans, corn, maple syrup, with oats and rye thrown in for diversion, it is a survivable farm if not exactly profitable, in fact probably closer to a religious experience than a proper vocation. This explains why otherwise sane children attempt the odd habit of agriculture. Caught up in the apostasy of the primitive who despite the chrome-plated altar of the orthodox, tend the worship of Nature, as is God in work clothes.

Justin Isherwood is an award-winning writer. He graduated from the University of Wisconsin-Stevens Point, went to United Theological Seminary, served as medical personnel during Vietnam, tried life in the passing lane with a tie on, then returned to the farm. With Lynn he built a house, raised two kids, studied trout, tended the fields and began writing. His books include *The Farm West of Mars, The Book of Plough,* and *White Ladies & Naked Gardens.* His writings have appeared in a variety of newspapers, magazines and collections.

He farms in Plover Township, on land that knew his great, great, great grandfathers . . . Ouicosee.